PRAISE FOR CH

Family Money

"The action barrels along to a shocking conclusion . . . Zunker knows how to keep the reader hooked."

—*Publishers Weekly*

An Equal Justice

HARPER LEE PRIZE FOR LEGAL FICTION FINALIST

"A deftly crafted legal thriller of a novel by an author with a genuine knack for a reader-engaging narrative storytelling style."

—Midwest Book Review

"A gripping thriller with a heart, *An Equal Justice* hits the ground running . . . The chapters flew by, with surprises aplenty and taut writing. A highly recommended read that introduces a lawyer with legs."

—Crime Thriller Hound

"In *An Equal Justice*, author Chad Zunker crafts a riveting legal thriller . . . *An Equal Justice* not only plunges readers into murder and conspiracy involving wealthy power players, but also immerses us in the crisis of homelessness in our country."

—*The Big Thrill*

"A thriller with a message. A pleasure to read. Twists I didn't see coming. I read it in one sitting."

—Robert Dugoni, #1 Amazon Charts bestselling author of *My Sister's Grave*

"Taut, suspenseful, and action-packed with a hero you can root for, Zunker has hit it out of the park with this one."

—Victor Methos, bestselling author of *The Neon Lawyer*

An Unequal Defense

"In Zunker's solid sequel to 2019's *An Equal Justice*, Zunker . . . sustains a disciplined focus on plot and character. John Grisham fans will appreciate this familiar but effective tale."

—*Publishers Weekly*

Runaway Justice

"[In the] engrossing third mystery featuring attorney David Adams . . . Zunker gives heart and hope to his characters. There are no lulls in this satisfying story of a young runaway in trouble."

—*Publishers Weekly*

ALL
HE
HAS
LEFT

ALSO BY CHAD ZUNKER

Family Money

David Adams Series

An Equal Justice
An Unequal Defense
Runaway Justice

Sam Callahan Series

The Tracker
Shadow Shepherd
Hunt the Lion

ALL HE HAS LEFT

CHAD ZUNKER

THOMAS & MERCER

Published by Thomas & Mercer, Seattle

www.apub.com

Amazon, the Amazon logo, and Thomas & Mercer are trademarks of Amazon.com, Inc., or its affiliates.

ISBN-13: 9781662504297 (paperback)
ISBN-13: 9781662504303 (digital)

Cover design by Rex Bonomelli
Cover image: © mammuth / Getty Images; © William Curtis Rolf / Gallery Stock

Printed in the United States of America

To my daughters, Anna, Madison, and Lexi

PROLOGUE

Jake Slater was already having a bad night. It would get much worse. Death changes everything. Especially when it hits as sudden as a devastating tornado.

Jake was not altogether shocked when he walked into the empty parking lot outside Stephen F. Austin High School, where he was the head football coach, and found the words *Coach Slater Sucks* spray-painted in red on the side of his white Jeep Cherokee. Hours earlier, Jake's football team had lost their fifth game in a row. The fans were irate. This was Texas. Football was king. This year's team had been projected to make a run at state. But Jake had ruined everything—according to the community—by kicking the star player off the team six weeks ago for punching a teammate in practice. Jake had never heard a crowd boo so loudly at the end of a game, which felt like the lowest point of his twenty-year coaching career.

His phone buzzed in his pocket. He pulled it out and read a text message from his wife, Sarah. We're at my parents' house. Can you meet us here?

Jake sighed. The last thing he wanted to do was go over to his in-laws' place tonight. He was already tired and frustrated. Having anything to do with his overbearing father-in-law right now would only exacerbate that. He was supposed to be meeting his wife and eleven-year-old daughter, Piper, at an IHOP restaurant down the street—a family tradition they'd started a couple of years ago after home games. These postgame dinners had unfortunately been miserable of late.

He texted her back. I'm exhausted. Can we just go home?

Sarah replied, Please, Jake. Just for a few minutes.

He growled under his breath. Fine.

Jake climbed into his Jeep and put the key in the ignition. The engine sputtered for several long seconds—as if trying to make up its mind about running tonight—before eventually starting. The old Jeep was on its last legs. Jake had been driving it forever, though Sarah had wanted him to get a new vehicle a long time ago. Something nice like her Lexus SUV. His wife had a lucrative career as a financial partner in her family's investment firm. It had afforded them some luxuries most other high school coaches didn't have—like living in a spacious new house in an affluent suburb in West Austin. But Jake didn't want to stand out in the parking lot among his assistant coaches, who all drove run-down vehicles. Nobody got rich coaching high school football. He'd married into it.

Driving out of downtown proper, where the high school was located along the shores of Lady Bird Lake—a stretch of the Colorado River that weaves beautifully through the city—Jake headed west. A few minutes later, he pulled into the gated driveway of his in-laws' massive estate. Their place sat along an exclusive private street on a hill overlooking the river, with a spectacular view of downtown. A real estate agent friend had told him years ago that every property on this street was worth more than $20 million. And Jake's in-laws had one of the biggest homes—which looked more like a Tuscan castle to him. Sitting on four acres, the house was over twelve thousand square feet. Everything about it seemed pretentious and ridiculous. His mother-in-law, Janice, might as well have left price tags on items she'd purchased from around the globe, the way she so casually talked about the expense of every statue, vase, and piece of artwork.

Jake punched in a code at the security gate, waited for it to open, and then drove up the winding path to the house. He parked next to Sarah's Lexus in a huge circular courtyard bordered by two four-bay garages on each side.

Jake walked up to the front door of the three-story mansion, with its mix of earth-toned stone and stucco, rustic lines, and beautiful arched openings and doorways. He knocked on the massive glass front door. His daughter answered it. Piper was the spitting image of her beautiful mother. Long brown hair pulled back in a tight ponytail with a few freckles on her cheeks and the brightest green eyes.

While she looked like her mother, Piper had the competitive drive and athletic ability of her father. Jake had played college football at Sam Houston State twenty years ago, where he'd broken several wide-receiver records. Piper competed nationally on a junior acrobatics and tumbling team. It was not uncommon for Piper to do a backflip while they were all just standing around. It drove Jake crazy. Board games between him and his daughter could get intense. He loved that about her. Being a father had given him an indescribable joy. Because of that, Jake had wanted more kids. But Sarah would never commit because of her busy career.

Piper immediately hugged him. "Sorry, Daddy."

He hugged her back, knowing she was talking about the game. "Thanks, baby."

"They played a lot better than last week. If not for that late fumble."

"I know. We'll get them next week. Where's Mom?"

"In the lounge with Grandpa."

Jake stepped fully into the three-story foyer with a sweeping staircase built in all marble that he knew had been imported from Italy. The house had always seemed more like a museum than a home. To him, it was cold and uncomfortable. Which could also describe his relationship with his father-in-law, Lars Kingston.

Jake followed Piper down a hallway to his left, which eventually spilled out into what the family called the lounge. It reminded Jake of a luxurious hotel lobby, with its multiple fireplaces and sitting areas. The entire Kingston family gathered here for every holiday and birthday celebration.

Sarah walked over to him, a glass of wine in her hand. She was a fit brunette who had run cross-country while attending Columbia back in the day. She still jogged nearly every morning before breakfast. Jake used to join her several days a week but not lately. He'd been leaving the house earlier than usual to put in more hours at the football offices and try to somehow rescue the season. Plus, he had been avoiding a growing tension between them. His body was paying for the lack of exercise—a slight softness around his belly that had not been there the first forty-two years of his life. There was also now a touch of gray in his wavy brown hair. Coaching could age a man quickly, especially when he was riding a serious losing streak.

"Hey," she said. "How're you holding up?"

"Tough night," he replied.

"Yeah. They've all been tough lately."

She said it without much warmth behind it. He could tell being a coach's wife was taking its toll on her. When they'd married thirteen years ago, she'd liked that he was just a normal guy with a salt-of-the-earth type of job working with kids. Sarah came from major wealth, and until that point had dated only guys who were born and bred in her pampered lifestyle. At the time, she'd wanted something different. They'd fallen for each other in that opposites-attract kind of way. But the pressure of mounting losses was also wearing on Sarah. She'd been getting yelled at herself during games while sitting in the stands. High school football could bring out the best and worst in people. They were currently living through the worst of it, but Jake knew it would pass. Growing up in a coaching family had taught him that.

Jake's father-in-law stood over by a fancy bar wrapped in colorful Italian tile. He had a glass undoubtedly filled with expensive Scotch in his hand. Wearing a black sweater and gray slacks, Lars was a physically imposing man at around six five with broad shoulders and a thick gray beard. Head of Kingston Financial, Lars liked to use his physical stature to intimidate others. But it had never worked on Jake, who at six two was only slightly shorter and still had his own set of muscular shoulders.

"Something to drink, Jake?" Lars asked him.

"Sure. I'll have what you're having."

Lars kind of scoffed. "This is from a ten-thousand-dollar bottle of Scotch. How about a beer instead?"

Jake barely hid rolling his eyes. From the first moment Sarah had brought him around, Lars had treated him as lower class—unworthy of drinking his expensive Scotch. Jake came from a poor family. Both his late father and grandfather had been high school football coaches like he was. There had never been any extra money around. Lars had clearly wanted his only daughter to marry someone from another wealthy family—just like her three older brothers had. Lars probably spent more money on new business suits each year than Jake made at coaching. Early on, Jake was convinced he could eventually win Lars over with his old-fashioned Southern charm. But that dream was dashed one fateful night when Jake unwittingly walked into the Kingston home and found Lars engaged in a sexual tryst with someone who was not his wife. Jake immediately bolted and never said a word to anyone. But he knew that Lars had seen him. From that point forward, Jake became a serious threat. And powerful men do not like to feel threatened. Lars clearly hated him for it.

"Actually, I don't need a drink," Jake said. "I just want to go home."

"I need a few minutes first," Lars insisted.

When Sarah invited Piper to join her in the kitchen to get a snack, Jake knew something was up. Sarah had been hinting at wanting a change for weeks. And now she'd pulled her damn father into it.

"What do you want?" he asked his father-in-law.

"To offer you a job opportunity."

"I don't need a job. I'm fine where I am."

"I can pay you five times what you're making right now."

"To do what?"

"I'm creating a new position within my company. Kind of like a mentor role for all first-year financial analysts. Life advice, counseling, guidance, that sort of thing."

"You want to pay me a half million dollars to babysit your new hires?"

He shrugged. "Something like that."

After thirteen years around his father-in-law, Jake was no longer surprised by the man's audacity. Money was the center of his entire world. Of course he thought Jake could simply be bought. "That's ridiculous."

Lars immediately frowned. "Don't be a fool, Jake. Sarah is not happy."

"That's between us. Not you."

"Apparently not, since she asked me to do this."

"So you just made up this position to get me out of coaching?"

"My daughter and granddaughter deserve better."

"Than being part of a coaching family? Or me?"

"Both," Lars said without hesitation, eyes narrow, sipping his Scotch.

"Thanks, but no thanks."

Jake felt a surge of anger push to the surface. He resisted the urge to let a few curse words fly and instead left the lounge in a hurry to go find Sarah and Piper. They were in the kitchen eating out of a tub of mint chocolate chip ice cream.

"I'm out of here," he snapped at Sarah, not hiding his irritation with her.

"Jake, wait," Sarah responded.

"I'll go with you, Daddy," Piper said, hopping up off her kitchen stool.

Piper hustled up to Jake's side in the hallway, reached out, and took his hand. While Sarah had become more distant during his current losing streak, Jake's daughter had drawn even closer to him, as if she knew her father needed the extra love and comfort right now. They had a special relationship. He hated that she'd been watching her mom and dad fight more than usual lately. A chasm was growing between her parents, and Jake wasn't sure how to resolve it. He'd never anticipated it reaching this point. They'd felt so united for most of their marriage. Life was good for them despite the hostility from his father-in-law. But the man was relentless. He was like the devil in Sarah's ear, constantly telling his daughter she could do better. This was a tug-of-war Jake felt like they'd easily won for more than thirteen years because Sarah was pulling along with him. Together, they were strong. But Sarah had not been pulling as hard lately. Which left Jake feeling betrayed.

"Jake, please, let's talk about this," Sarah said, chasing after him.

"Not tonight. Later."

"You always say that but never want to talk about it later."

"Sarah, I'm tired. I don't want to say things I'll regret."

Jake walked out the front door with Piper. Sarah was right behind them.

"I'm tired, too, Jake," Sarah said. "Tired of all of this. That's why we must talk about it right now. Aren't you fed up?"

"We've been through these tough times before."

"Yeah, I know, and it *never* ends. It's like a vicious cycle. I'm really starting to hate everything about football."

Sarah wanted to fight tonight. But he didn't. Not in front of Piper.

"Daddy, your car!" Piper gasped, stopping to stare at the red spray-painted graffiti.

"It's no big deal."

"Real nice," Sarah said, rolling her eyes. "This is exactly my point."

"Jeez, Dad," Piper added. "You don't suck. People suck."

"Sometimes they do," he agreed. "Let's go."

They both climbed into his Jeep. But this time when Jake turned the key in the ignition, the engine just kept sputtering without ever starting. Then it died altogether. Jake pounded his fist against the steering wheel, feeling so angry about tonight, about the football season, about what had just happened with his father-in-law, and about the dire feeling that his family was slowly falling apart.

Piper reached over, put her small hand on his arm. "Daddy, calm down. It's going to be okay."

"I know," he said. "We just need to let it sit for a second and try again."

"No, Daddy. I mean *everything* is going to be okay."

Jake looked over, stared at his daughter. She gave him a reassuring smile, one that wrinkled up her cute little nose, and he could feel his anger slowly begin to dissipate.

"Sun will come out tomorrow, right?" Piper added.

He grinned at her. This was something he always said to her when she was devastated after one of her meets did not go well. She was turning it back on him when he really needed it.

"Yes, it will," he agreed. "You're my whole world, you know that?"

She grinned sheepishly.

"I mean it," Jake said. "I love you very much."

"I love you, too, Daddy."

Minutes later, Jake was driving Sarah's Lexus SUV as they all headed home together. He would send a tow truck to retrieve his Jeep in the morning. The streets were dark and quiet. It was after midnight. He glanced in the rearview mirror. Piper had her earbuds in and was listening to music. Sarah sat quietly and mostly stared out the passenger window. Jake pulled to a halt at a stoplight.

"I'm sorry, Sarah. I know this is hard."

She turned. "I'm sorry, too. I just don't know what to do anymore."

"We'll figure it out. I promise."

Jake started to ease the vehicle into the intersection. A split second later, he saw a flash of bright headlights appear right outside Sarah's passenger window, approaching them rapidly. It looked like a large truck of some kind. And it wasn't slowing down. He felt a surge of panic rush through him. Jake had no time to hit the gas and get out of the way. He cursed, instinctively put his right arm out to brace Sarah, protectively yelled out Piper's name because that's all he could do. Then he felt the explosion of metal and glass, his body jerking with a force he'd never experienced, the SUV suddenly being lifted into the air and twisting sideways, like a scary amusement-park ride. His head whipped back and forth as airbags filled the vehicle. They were flipping over and over—he couldn't tell how many times. His chest felt like it was being crushed by the fierce tug of the tight seatbelt.

More twisting, flipping, crunching.

Then everything suddenly settled.

Jake could tell they were right side up but couldn't see anything at first. His eyes were unable to focus. But he could smell a horrible mix of oil and gas and rubber burning. And he could hear the hissing of burst valves and pipes in the vehicle's engine. He was surprised to find himself alert. His face felt like it was on fire. He reached up and touched his cheek and then stared blurry-eyed at his hand. Things gradually came into semifocus. His fingers were covered in blood. *Piper!* He turned his neck, which hurt like hell, to look for his daughter in the back seat. She was hunched over and kind of lying limp, like she was being held up by only her seat belt. Jake felt more panic. Then his daughter jerked back upright and moaned loudly. She was at least alive. But what about Sarah?

Jake pivoted to look over at his wife, who was pinned up against him from the full impact of the collision against the passenger door. He felt a wave of horror rip through him. Her arms and legs were twisted and crushed. Blood was everywhere. Her eyes were open and looking at him, but there was something hollow about them. And she wasn't moving. He tried to say something to her but couldn't seem to get any words out. Was his throat damaged? He reached over with his right hand, grabbed her arm, gently tugged. But she didn't respond. It only made her head drop limply.

Jake felt his whole world sucking in on him, like a dizzying spiral. What could he do? He couldn't move. Jake glanced up through the shattered windshield and thought he saw the shadow of a man standing directly in front of their vehicle. He couldn't make out the man's face. The guy was just staring at them but not really doing anything. Why wasn't the man trying to help them? Had he at least called 911? Then the man turned and hurried off. Jake blinked a couple of times. Was he only seeing things?

More spiraling. He started gasping.

Was he dying?

Was Sarah already gone?

Was Piper going to make it?

Then everything went completely black.

ONE

After making the two-hour drive to Austin, Jake finally pulled his Jeep Cherokee into the gated driveway of his in-laws' estate around noon on a Saturday in early November. The leaves had started to turn, and a nice chill was hanging in the air. Jake had hated coming here during his marriage with Sarah and tried to avoid it whenever possible. He hadn't been back since she'd died a year ago. Not that his in-laws wanted him here, either. His father-in-law had directly blamed him for their daughter's tragic death, even though all the police reports pointed toward a no-fault hit-and-run accident. Dealing with his in-laws over the past year had been a much bigger nightmare for him than the sum of all the years before that.

If it weren't for Piper, Jake never would have spoken to them again.

His daughter sat quietly in the passenger seat next to him. Although she wouldn't give him the pleasure of knowing it, Jake could tell she was happy about getting to spend her thirteenth birthday with friends and family. They hadn't been back to Austin since he'd packed them up four months ago and moved them into the old house his father had left for him in Simonton—a small town of less than a thousand outside Houston, where Jake had grown up.

Jake had to get away from Sarah's parents and try to start over. They had put him through a brutal custody battle for Piper in the aftermath of Sarah's death. In the darkest moment of Jake's life, Lars Kingston had chosen to leverage every bit of his money and power to prove to the courts that Jake was an unfit father and Piper would be better off living with them. Jake might have had many problems dealing with Sarah's death—some more serious than others, he'd admit—but he was still a good father. For Lars to use such a difficult time to make an opportunistic play for Piper was incredibly cruel—even for him. In a desperate response, Jake had finally played a card with Lars he'd held on to for more than a decade. He threatened to expose the affair he'd stumbled upon many years ago. Jake had recognized the woman. She was the wife of a prominent politician. Jake knew word leaking out, even years later, would cause serious havoc for his father-in-law. Not only could it jeopardize his in-laws' marriage, but it might potentially have devastating consequences for Kingston Financial. Lars erupted on him with a rage he'd never seen before ultimately backing down.

Nevertheless, Jake couldn't keep Piper away from his in-laws forever. Like it or not, they were still her grandparents.

Jake waited for the automatic metal gate to open in front of them. "You excited?" he asked Piper.

She gave a quick nod but didn't say anything. The entire drive had been pretty quiet, no matter how much he'd tried to initiate conversation. Of course, it had been this way between them for the better part of the past year and had grown only worse since he'd forced her to leave her friends behind in Austin.

Although she'd never said it to him directly, Jake knew Piper also partly blamed him for her mother's death. She'd been in the car watching them argue that night. In many ways, he blamed himself. It was impossible not to wonder if he could have done something differently.

Jake had replayed the moment repeatedly in his mind. Had he not been paying attention when he'd pulled into the intersection? Was it still a red light? Had he been distracted by his own anger at Sarah? Unfortunately, Jake would never get those questions answered. Whoever had hit them with the speeding truck had disappeared before anyone else arrived. And the police were never able to track them down.

Jake hated that his once-special relationship with his daughter had been so severely damaged this past year but felt determined to somehow get it back. Which was why he'd had the idea to bring her here for her birthday. When the gate fully opened, he pulled up the driveway to the house and parked in the huge circular courtyard. Two white cargo trucks were also parked in front of the house, and various workers were busy lifting out tables and chairs and what looked like other assorted party decorations. Jake was not surprised his in-laws were going over the top for this birthday celebration. He resented them for continuing to use their money to buy his daughter's affection.

Jake felt his stomach twist when he spotted his mother-in-law, Janice, appear on the front porch. Per usual, her dyed black hair was dolled up perfectly. She wore a white silk blouse, black dress pants, and heels. Jake could see her diamond jewelry sparkling in the midday sun. There had never been anything casual about Janice. Seconds later, the man he now despised more than anyone in the world stepped out behind her. Lars Kingston. Jake felt the rage immediately bubble up inside him. But he knew he had to somehow play nice for Piper's sake. He wasn't going to ruin this for her.

They got out of his Jeep. He watched as Piper hurried over to them, limping slightly with each step. The car wreck had badly fractured her left leg, and doctors still weren't sure if she'd ever be able to compete in acro-tumbling again. She'd been doing intense physical therapy for the past year, but progress had been excruciatingly slow. His daughter had lost more than just her mother.

He watched as his daughter hugged both of her grandparents. Then he made his way up to the front of the house. Jake exchanged a quick but cold-natured nod with Lars. Janice gave him a fake hug and a kiss on the cheek, as if everything were normal, as if she hadn't testified to the judge about him being a horrible father only six months ago. Jake felt his whole chest tightening and knew he needed to make an exit as soon as possible.

"Piper, I'll be back to get you later tonight," he told his daughter.

"Are you sure you can't stay?" she asked.

Jake gave a quick glance at Lars. His ice-cold gaze told him he was clearly not welcome at this party. Not that Jake wanted to stay, anyway.

"No, you have fun," he replied. "I have some things I have to take care of around town while we're here."

Piper walked back over and hugged him tightly. In his ear, she whispered, "Thank you, Daddy. I really mean it."

Considering how hot and cold things were between them at the moment, her words meant a lot to him. "You're welcome, baby."

"Come on, honey," Janice said to Piper. "I want to show you the giant chocolate fountain I had brought in just for you and your friends. I also have a new dress for you. My gal will be here to do your hair and makeup in about twenty minutes. We need to get you ready because our guests will arrive soon."

Jake's mother-in-law ushered his daughter inside the house, leaving him standing there with his father-in-law.

"She can stay the night with us," Lars said. "You don't have to come back."

"No, she can't."

"That's ridiculous. We have a full guest suite."

"She'll stay with me at the hotel."

"You're being petty, you know that?"

"Petty would've been not allowing her to come here at all."

Lars moved his jaw around, like he wanted to say something but resisted. The man was used to controlling everyone in his life. But he had never been able to control Jake. And that had always annoyed him.

"You working again yet?" he asked Jake.

"That's not really your concern."

"My granddaughter is my concern. Not you."

"Yeah, you've made that very clear."

"I know you're *not* working. Piper told Janice over the phone."

"Then why the hell did you ask?"

"So how exactly are you providing for Piper?"

"We're getting by just fine, thanks."

Truthfully, things were a bit tight. Jake hadn't drawn a paycheck since his high school had fired him eleven months ago. Not a lot of schools wanted to hire a coach who had drunkenly tried to choke a ref on the sideline during a game. Jake had gotten sober during the custody battle.

Lars kept pressing. "It doesn't have to be this hard. Just let the child come live with us. You know we'll take tremendous care of her."

"Are we really doing this again right now?"

"Piper needs to be with her family."

He gritted his teeth. "She *is* with her family."

"You know what I'm saying. We can give her what you can't. The best schools, the best physical therapy, the best of everything. She doesn't have to live in some shack in the middle of nowhere away from all of us."

"It's not a shack."

Jake wanted to take a swing at the man. His father had helped build the house where they were currently living with his own hands.

"Whatever." Lars grunted. "Don't keep her there just to spite us."

Jake turned to walk away. "Enjoy your party."

"You're making her miserable," Lars continued. "That's what she tells Janice. Your own daughter hates you. She wants to be with us."

He didn't respond, just kept walking. Responding would only escalate things. In some bizarre way, Lars had felt entitled to Piper after losing his only daughter. As if taking possession of her were the fair replacement for Sarah. He'd become obsessed with it. Maybe it was his own way of dealing with the insufferable pain. Jake had tried to be somewhat understanding early on.

"What's it going to take, Jake?" Lars shouted after him. "A million? Is that what you want? How about five million?"

Jake got in his car, took a deep breath. Every part of him wanted to get back out and confront his father-in-law. The man was ruthless to his core. But if Jake got out, things might actually turn physical. And then Jake probably would lose his daughter in court. Maybe that was Lars's plan today. Was he trying to entice a physical response out of him? The man was relentless.

Jake started his car and quickly drove away.

TWO

Eddie Cowens had never been seriously incarcerated—not like his deadbeat father, who'd spent the first five years of Eddie's life in prison for burglary. But Eddie had seen a good amount of local jail time in his twenty-eight years for various misdemeanors. He blamed most of his troubles on his father—or lack thereof. His dad had bolted on him and his younger sister when he was only thirteen after the police had come around asking about a truckload of stolen electronics. He'd overheard his father once talk about disappearing across the Texas-Mexico border and never coming back. Eddie hadn't seen or heard from the man since. So he'd become the man of the family at an early age and did his best to take care of his little sister, Beth—especially since his mom was wasted half the time. The old lady had been a drunk long before his father had ever left. Not that Eddie really blamed her. That's just the way it was for them, living the dirt-poor trailer-park life here on the outskirts of East Austin.

But things had been much better for everyone of late—thanks to his whip-smart sister. Beth had put herself in a promising position to take care of them, maybe for the rest of their lives. Their bills were all paid, for the first time in forever. He was driving a newer truck. Plenty of cash for food and fun. Life was damn good at the moment. But all of it was suddenly being threatened, according to the old lady—what he called his mother. She'd texted him twenty minutes ago and told him to get over to the trailer ASAP.

Eddie pulled his black truck onto the dirt road of the trailer park, kicking dust up all around him with his oversize tires. One of the neighbors near the front shouted at him. Eddie gave him the middle finger in return. He circled around to the back and then jerked to a stop in front of the old lady's run-down RV—the dump where he and Beth were both raised. He'd slept on the short and stiff couch every night while Beth shared the only bed with their mother.

Getting out of his truck, Eddie straightened his black trucker cap, flicked his joint into the dirt by his scuffed cowboy boots. The sun was beginning to set over his left shoulder. He made eyes at the teenage girl who was standing out front watering flowers on the porch of another RV next door. She was a real looker but couldn't be more than fifteen. He knew the girl lived with her fat mother, who used a wheelchair. What was the girl's name again? Allison? Ali? He was too high to remember at the moment. The girl smiled awkwardly at him and then went back inside her trailer. Eddie had always had a way with the ladies. He liked them young, too. The younger girls wouldn't give him as much lip. Girls his own age had way too much attitude.

Walking up to the old lady's door, Eddie pounded on it.

"Get your ass in here!" he heard his mom shout from inside.

He opened the door, stepped into the small quarters. There was a tiny bedroom on one end, a kitchen in the middle, and a living space at the opposite end. His mom now kept it neat and tidy, but that hadn't always been the case. There was a row of empty liquor bottles lined up on the kitchen counter next to the sink. Some things never changed, even with an influx of money. More cash simply meant more booze. The old lady was only fifty-two, but she looked more like she was sixtysomething. Her frizzy hair was mostly gray, her skin weathered. She sat in a chair next to the TV with a cigarette in one hand and a glass of whiskey in the other. Probably Jim Beam. His mom loved her cheap whiskey. Eddie noticed she had on her favorite black Van Halen tank top. She wore that damn shirt nearly every day.

Eddie walked straight to the fridge, grabbed a beer from inside, popped it open. "What's wrong, Mom? What the hell is so important you couldn't just tell me on the phone? I'm busy."

"Doing what? Stealing cars with that moron, Jason?"

"I got real jobs, too, you know."

Eddie had been driving a tow truck part-time for a couple of years. Beth had also been getting him some work lately. He was doing all right. The car-stealing stuff was just for weekend kicks with the boys.

"We got a real problem, Edward."

Eddie eyeballed her over his beer can. She only called him *Edward* when it was something serious. "What?"

"Where were you this afternoon?"

"Doing some setup stuff for Beth's company. Why?"

The old lady cursed.

"What the hell is wrong?" Eddie asked.

"She recognized you."

"Who?"

"That damn little birthday girl. That's who."

Eddie cursed this time. "No way."

"She even took a photo of you. Beth said questions were being asked."

"By who?"

"I don't know exactly. But it ain't good."

"Does anyone know I'm Beth's brother?"

The old lady shrugged. "I don't think so. Not yet. But we've got to do something right now before it ever gets that far."

"Like what?"

"Shut people up."

"How do you expect me to do that?"

"You still got your daddy's gun?"

"Are you serious?"

"You want to lose everything? You want to go to prison just like your daddy? For the first time in our lives, we actually have some kind of future ahead of us. Hell, Beth said she wants me to go look at houses with her tomorrow. Can you believe that? A real house for me, Eddie. Maybe even a little yard for a garden. But it may all go away if you don't go take care of this situation right now."

"This is crazy."

"I'm not telling you to shoot anyone. I'm just saying, you know, scare them."

Eddie cursed again, pulled out another joint.

"Don't smoke that right now, you idiot!" the old lady berated him. "You need to be thinking clearly tonight."

She was right. He put it away. "Where's Beth?"

"I don't know. But she said to call her as soon as you leave here."

"Fine," he huffed. "I'll take care of it."

"Tonight, Edward. Or this could be over for all of us by tomorrow."

THREE

Jake planned to pick up Piper around eight that evening. He'd made special dinner reservations for them downtown at Truluck's. When Sarah was alive and they were still a family, their yearly tradition was having Piper's birthday dinner at the fancy restaurant followed by stuffing themselves on gourmet doughnuts at Gourdough's on South Lamar. Piper's favorite had always been the Funky Monkey, a giant doughnut with cream cheese icing, topped with grilled caramelized bananas and loads of brown sugar. Jake and Piper had not partaken in this activity last year since they were still reeling in the aftermath of Sarah's death. Jake was hoping to find some happy ground again. Although he wondered how hard it would be for them to do this without Sarah.

His wife's death still didn't feel real to him—even a year later. There was a lingering numbness there. Probably because he never really gave himself much of a chance to work through the emotional pain. First, he went back to coaching way too soon and was subsequently fired after embarrassing himself in front of hundreds of fans. Then the custody battle put him through the emotional wringer. But Jake felt like he had been making slow progress over the past couple of months. He'd hoped this weekend would be a big step forward for both him and Piper in many ways.

After exchanging texts with Piper, Jake knew she'd spent the past hour after her birthday party had ended over at her favorite cousin's house. Caitlin had been his daughter's primary babysitter for most of her life. She was the daughter of Sarah's oldest brother, Carl. Even with a ten-year age gap between them, the two girls had a special bond. Caitlin was a newly working professional after graduating from Stanford a few months ago. She had just moved into a fabulous modern two-story white house only a couple of blocks north of Lake Austin near downtown—something she could never afford on her own. Lars Kingston had purchased it for her as a college graduation gift.

When Jake had graduated from Sam Houston State, he'd had to move back into his old bedroom at his father's house. It took six months of collecting paychecks from his first low-paying coaching gig before he finally got himself into an efficiency apartment. Caitlin had moved straight into a multimillion-dollar neighborhood. Not that Jake held that against his niece. This was just normal for her family. He actually respected that Caitlin had not chosen the easy path of going directly to work for her grandfather, like most others in her family. She had studied criminal justice in college and was carving out her own unique path within the field of law enforcement.

Jake pulled his Jeep to the curb outside the house. A sporty black Audi was parked in the side driveway. Piper had texted him a photo of Caitlin's car earlier and said she wanted one just like it when she got her license in a few years. She added a huge smiley-face emoji. In their brief text exchanges throughout the afternoon, Piper had used a *lot* of happy emojis. It made his heart feel good. Jake had given her a brand-new phone this morning for her birthday—something she'd been begging for. The gift seemed to have opened a positive communication line between them. At least for one day. He hoped it would last.

Getting out of his car, he took a quick glance up and down the picturesque street, which was lined with similarly exquisite houses. He noticed a woman out walking her dog to his left. Two teenagers on motorized scooters farther down. A tow truck parked on the street a half block to his right. Zipping up his black windbreaker, Jake followed the walking path to the front porch of the house. Right before he was about to knock on the door, a sudden loud *bang!* from inside jarred him and sent a chill straight up his spine.

What the hell was that? A gunshot? Then Jake thought he heard a female shriek from somewhere inside the house, and panic punched him in the gut.

Jake pounded hard on the front door.

"Hey, it's Uncle Jake! Is everything OK?"

No response. Jake cursed, glanced through a small window right next to the front door, but he couldn't see anyone in the foyer of the house. He reached down for the door handle but found it locked.

He again pounded on the door. "Caitlin! Piper!"

Still no one came to answer. His heart was racing. He hurried over to his left in front of a window on the opposite end of the porch. The lights were on in the living room, but he couldn't make out anyone inside the house. Another scream. His adrenaline hit another level. Without even thinking twice, Jake reared back and punched his jacket-covered elbow right through the glass window. It shattered. He quickly cleared glass shards away as best he could without cutting himself and then managed to climb through the opening over the top of a white sofa. He scrambled toward the back of the house, the source of the commotion.

Spinning around a corner, Jake spotted his niece lying on her back on the hardwood floor in the kitchen, clutching her stomach with both hands and gasping for air. It looked like her hands were covered in blood. He could see dark liquid collecting beneath Caitlin. Jake dropped to his knees next to his niece, feeling more and more panic grip him. Blood was flowing out of her stomach, so he instinctively put his own hands on top of hers to try to somehow stop it. It wasn't working. Blood was everywhere.

"Caitlin? What happened?"

"P-p-p-iper," she said, coughing up more blood.

"She did this to you?" Jake said, horrified.

"N-n-no. He . . . he did it."

"Who? Is he here?"

"She knows, Uncle Jake. What happened wasn't an accident."

"What . . . Who knows?"

Caitlin began coughing up more blood. "Piper knows the truth."

"Where is she?"

"Help her, Uncle Jake! Please!"

Jake reached his trembling hand into his pocket to find his phone. He had to call 911. He had to get paramedics here for Caitlin. She was in awful condition. But then he heard another scream come from right outside the house. One he'd recognize anywhere. Pressing off the floor, Jake raced for a back kitchen door that led out to the side driveway. He flung it open, spilled outside, frantically searching everywhere. He didn't see anything in a small backyard to his left, so he sprinted forward around to the front of the house again.

Where was Piper? *God, please!* he kept thinking, fear gripping his whole body. Squinting up the dark street, Jake thought he saw a man push someone into the front seat of the black tow truck he'd noticed parked along the curb earlier. *Piper!* A second later, the man pulled the truck door shut behind him.

The engine roared to life. Jake took off running after it. The tires squealed on the pavement, and the tow truck roared away from him, taking a swift right at the next cross street. Jake had to somehow get to the truck before it got away.

He ran up the same street as the truck, pumping his legs as hard as possible, but he was quickly losing ground. He had to find another way. The truck skidded around a corner up ahead of him. Peering to his right, Jake decided his only chance was to cut up a side street, hoping he might be able to intercept the truck. He heard the truck's tires squeal again. At the next cross street, Jake cut through a yard on the corner. But then he found himself approaching a waist-high picket fence. Without slowing, Jake tried to hurtle the fence with one explosive leap but caught his front left foot instead. He toppled over the fence and landed square on his face on the opposite sidewalk. He thought he felt something crack in his jaw. Pushing himself up, he stumbled forward, back into the street, kept on running. But the tow truck was already in the distance. Within seconds, he could no longer see the taillights. Whoever had his daughter was long gone.

Jake fell to his knees, gasping for breath. *God, no!* Then he heard police sirens swiftly approaching. *Caitlin!*

FOUR

A police car with lights flashing was already parked in front of Caitlin's house when Jake raced back down the sidewalk. He could hear more sirens approaching from nearby streets. A neighbor must've heard the gunshot and called the police. *Thank God.* Jake was desperate for help. He tried hard to not think about Piper being inside that truck, frightened out of her mind. But it was impossible for him. Had she been in the kitchen when Caitlin had been shot? Had she seen it happen right in front of her? Was Piper also hurt? Jake felt a swirling of panic inside and could hardly think or breathe. He was so confused. What had happened? Who had taken Piper?

Jake rushed up to the front of the house, searching for a police officer to help him. As he did, a uniformed officer suddenly stepped out of the front door. Spotting Jake's swift approach, the officer drew his gun, yelled, "Stop right there!" Jake immediately put his hands up, which he now noticed were completely covered in blood. He looked down and saw that blood was all over his jacket, too. He must've wiped his hands on his jacket while he hovered over Caitlin.

"Officer, please, my daughter was just taken! A man just shot my niece inside and took my daughter in a black tow truck. Please help me!"

"Sir, drop to your knees *right now*, and keep your hands up!"

Jake did what he was told. "Officer, *please*, the man is getting away! You have to do something right now! Please, God. Help me! *Do something!*"

The officer hesitantly approached. "Do you have ID on you, sir?"

Jake nodded. "Yes, in my front pocket. My name is Jake Slater. My daughter is Piper. She's only thirteen."

"Slowly pull out your ID for me."

Jake carefully reached into his jean pocket. "Officer, are you even listening to me? You're wasting time! Please help me!"

"I will!" the officer sternly yelled back. "Just stay put, and give me a second."

Jake handed over his wallet. The officer opened it, began examining Jake's driver's license. Another police car arrived, siren blazing, lights flashing. Two more officers ran up the sidewalk with guns drawn. The young officer who held his wallet quickly updated them. *911 call. Gunshot heard. Man spotted running from house. Woman down inside the kitchen.* Then the officer nodded at Jake.

"He says his daughter was taken."

"She was!" Jake yelled. "And they're going to get away unless one of you does something *right now!*"

"What's with all the blood?" asked one of the officers.

Jake's chest was pounding so hard, he could barely breathe. "I got here a few minutes ago to pick up my daughter. She was with my niece. That's the girl inside the house. Caitlin Kingston. I heard a gunshot and broke in through the front window. I found my niece on the kitchen floor. I tried to stop her bleeding." Jake was gasping for breath. "Then I heard my daughter scream from outside the house. I took off running after them. I saw a man push her into a black tow truck and speed away."

"Did you recognize this man?" asked the same officer who mentioned the blood.

"No, I didn't get a good look at him. I just . . ."

Jake felt a sudden surge of emotion exploding from the depth of his bowels and vomited on the sidewalk in front of him. He could feel his whole world collapsing. Piper was all he had left. He heard one of the officers on his radio saying something about a potential child kidnapping and a black tow truck. At least they were finally responding to his desperate pleas. Then an officer who had been inside the house stepped onto the front porch. Jake looked up and noticed the grim expression on his face and felt another knot twist up in his stomach.

"Gunshot wound to the stomach," the officer explained to the others. "She's already dead."

Jake pressed his bloodied hands to his face. "No!"

FIVE

Jake sat on a curb next to a police car, where he was being steadily monitored by the same young officer who had drawn his gun on him earlier. He was trying to somehow hold it together but was having difficulty processing all this and felt his panic growing. There had been no further updates from anyone about the pursuit of a black tow truck and Piper's potential whereabouts. Because Jake had just given Piper her new phone with a new account this morning, he hadn't taken any time to set up the phone's monitoring systems yet. He had no way of tracking her location through her phone's GPS. Each passing minute without her recovery felt like a weighted blanket being pressed down more heavily on him.

An ambulance had arrived on the scene along with several other emergency vehicles. It was like a scene from a movie, but this was crazy real. For the first time, Jake tried to process what Caitlin had said to him while he was inside the house. *What happened wasn't an accident. Piper knows the truth.* What did she mean? What truth? Could Piper have known the man who did this? Jake had explained all this to a detective, who took down his entire story in detail just a few minutes ago. But the conversation made him feel uneasy. Jake felt suspiciously eyeballed by the man the entire time. Was it possible the detective didn't believe him?

Within fifteen minutes, Jake's shocked in-laws began arriving at the chaotic scene. Jake watched at a distance as Caitlin's parents, Carl and Lisa, received the devastating news about their daughter. Jake thought Lisa might pass out. Carl just stood there with a stoic look on his face. More of Sarah's family showed up. Jake's brother-in-law Nicholas and his wife, Wendy, followed quickly by Jake's other brother-in-law, Steve. All of them lived in luxury homes close by. The family huddled together in the driveway with looks of absolute horror all over their faces. Finally, Lars and Janice arrived. Jake stood, wanting to speak to Lars, hoping his father-in-law could get the police to respond more aggressively to Piper's situation. For once, Jake wanted to be able to use the man's power and influence in his favor. They had to do *something* to find Piper.

"Where're you going?" the young officer asked.

"To speak with my father-in-law."

"You need to stay put," the officer instructed.

"Why? What the hell is going on?"

"Just stay where you are for now, sir."

Jake watched as the detective he'd spoken with a few minutes ago stood in the middle of the family huddle. An animated discussion was going on among all of them. Jake received several looks, but no one bothered to head over to him. Had they been instructed by the detective not to speak to him? He could see Lars looking in his direction with eyes like slits and his jaw set hard.

Finally, the detective—a fiftysomething man with a thick mustache wearing a tattered brown sport coat—came back over to the officer who had been watching Jake. "Put Mr. Slater in the car for now."

"What?" Jake exclaimed. "Am I being arrested?"

"Not yet. Just detained. Still gathering information."

"This is ridiculous. I'd like to speak to my wife's family."

"That's not going to happen right now."

"Why the hell not?"

"Let's just say they're not all convinced of your innocence."

"You've got to be kidding me!"

"Look, I haven't been able to corroborate your story about a man in a tow truck. And according to your father-in-law, you've had lots of issues lately. He claims you were angry at the woman inside because of some family custody battle."

"This has nothing to do with that!"

"Then we'll get it sorted out, Mr. Slater. For now, just sit tight."

"But what about my daughter?"

"We're already doing everything we can with that."

"It doesn't feel like it."

The detective motioned at the officer, who opened the back door to the police car and asked Jake to get inside. Jake was shocked. How could anyone from Sarah's family believe he might have had something to do with any of this? He wanted a chance to walk over and explain himself to his in-laws and beg them to help with Piper's pursuit. But he reluctantly complied, realizing that fighting with the officer was not going to get him anywhere except put in handcuffs. The officer shut the car door behind him and then drifted up the sidewalk about ten feet to speak with another officer.

Jake looked down and noticed there were no door handles in the back of the police car. He ran his fingers through his hair and then tugged on it out of frustration. He rubbed at his jaw, which was throbbing in pain from his fall. But thankfully, it didn't feel like anything was actually broken. Peering out the window, Jake felt completely helpless. He could see a group of neighbors standing on the opposite sidewalk, taking in all the drama, and thought about what the detective had just said. No one had seen the black tow truck? None of them had heard the truck tearing through the neighborhood? That seemed unlikely. Someone had to have seen *something*.

Jake was startled by his phone suddenly vibrating in his front left blue jean pocket. The police had taken his wallet—and still had it—but they had not asked for his phone. Pulling it out, he squinted at it and felt his heart jolt. *Piper!* A cute profile picture of her in her green-and-black acro-tumbling uniform filled his screen.

He quickly answered it. "Baby! Are you OK?"

There was no response. Just dead air.

"Piper, are you there?"

Again, she didn't say anything. But Jake could suddenly hear someone else speaking, although it sounded muffled and from a distance. He cupped the phone closely to his ear, listening as carefully as he could. It sounded like a man and a woman. Was Piper in the room with them? What was going on?

Man: "What the hell was I supposed to do? I couldn't just leave her there!"

Woman: "I told you just to scare them, you idiot. Not to shoot anyone!"

Man: "It was an accident. Stupid woman went for my gun. It just went off."

Woman: "This is bad. So very bad."

Man: "I knew I shouldn't have gone over there."

Woman: "All right, look, we just gotta calm down a second and think."

Man: "I need to talk to Beth. Tell her what's going on."

Woman: "No, no . . . not yet. She's going to completely freak out."

Man: "We can't just let her talk to her boss like nothing happened."

Woman: "Let me figure out a plan."

Man: "It's your damn plan that got us into this mess in the first place."

Woman: "Don't you talk to me that way!"

Man (sighing): "What the hell do I do with the girl?"

Woman: "We keep her in the barn until we figure this out. She could provide some kind of leverage for us if this goes really bad."

Man: "What if the police come around asking questions?"

A long pause.

Woman: "Then we do what we gotta do with her."

Oh God. Jake could feel his heart pumping so fast.

Woman: "Hey, take your hands out of your pockets." The woman's voice had grown louder, as if she were getting closer to the location of Piper's phone. "Damn it! Give me that!"

"Daddy!" Jake heard Piper yell.

Then the phone line went dead.

SIX

Jake stared wide-eyed at the phone in his shaky fingers.

What if the police come around asking questions?

Then we do what we gotta do with her.

The woman's words sent a chill to his core. He tried to push the overwhelming panic out of his mind for a moment and replay everything he could about the brief conversation between the two people. They were holding Piper in a barn somewhere. The woman had a raspy smoker's voice. The man sounded younger, but he couldn't be sure—Jake hadn't gotten a good look at the guy who'd climbed into the tow truck. The two people talked in a way that told him they were very familiar with each other. Husband and wife? Something else? They had mentioned someone's name: Beth. But this didn't trigger anything for him. Jake didn't know any Beth. They couldn't be too far away with Piper. It had been only thirty minutes since he'd watched the truck disappear.

They clearly had not known about Piper's phone. His daughter had put it in her back pocket this morning, so they probably hadn't noticed it. Piper must've somehow pulled it out, placed the call to him, and then put her hands in her hoodie's front pockets along with the phone. That was an incredibly brave thing for her to do. This meant she was thinking on her feet—which was encouraging. Although he wished she'd called 911. But she'd put her hope in her father instead. Hearing her yell out *Daddy!* was a dagger straight to his heart.

Jake again thought about what Caitlin had said earlier. *What happened wasn't an accident.* Was she talking about being shot? He shook his head. Clearly, that wasn't an accident. She had to be referring to something else. Could it be connected to her job at the FBI? Caitlin had just started working there in a low-level administrative role. But if it was FBI related, then how would Piper know anything about it? The man on the phone had said it was the woman's *plan* that had gotten them into this mess in the first place. That suddenly struck him a bit differently. Could Caitlin possibly have been talking about the hit-and-run *accident?* Did Piper know some kind of truth about that? Could these people somehow be connected to what had happened last year? His head began swirling. If the crash wasn't an accident, who would've wanted to intentionally harm him and his family? Jake found himself going back to the night of the crash, something a therapist had encouraged him to stop doing in order to allow himself to start healing. But he had no choice now.

There had been a lot of people around that time who were angry at him—but one person stood out from the rest: Judd McGee, the father of Quinn McGee, the star quarterback whom Jake had kicked off the football team. Judd was a burly man who worked in an auto shop; he always had grease on his shirts and pants, and alcohol all over his breath. Judd had come to a couple of practices in the weeks after his son was removed from the team, trying to ruffle feathers with intoxicated threats, talking about how Jake was ruining his kid's future. Jake had always kept his cool and defused each situation. But could Judd have snapped in a drunken rage a year ago? Judd likely had access to a tow truck. But then why would all this have suddenly resurfaced tonight? Why would he have taken Piper a year after the car crash?

Jake didn't know but felt eager to talk to Judd and get some answers. However, he was in a difficult position. Should he tell the detective about this conversation? The man was clearly skeptical of everything he'd said so far. Talking to him again could waste precious time since the detective might not believe him anyway. Plus, if the police got too close, these people had made their intentions very clear—they were going to kill Piper. Jake thought he could probably track down Judd McGee quickly. That might lead him straight to Piper. He had to get the hell out of there right now. He might be Piper's only chance. But how? He was locked in the back of a damn police car. And no one in a uniform seemed too eager to let him walk away from this crime scene anytime soon.

Still, he had to do something. He couldn't just sit there.

Jake started to knock loudly on the car window, trying to get the attention of the young officer outside. At first, the guy didn't turn around. So Jake pounded even harder on the glass. Finally, the officer turned back with a furrowed brow. Jake started frantically waving him over. The officer made his way to the car and opened the door a crack.

"What is it?"

"I think I'm going to be sick again," Jake lied. "I might vomit and didn't want to do it in the back of your car."

"Yeah, I appreciate that. Get out."

Jake pushed himself out of the vehicle. "OK if I go over there?" He motioned toward the grass up the sidewalk.

The officer nodded. "Just keep it off the sidewalk."

Holding his stomach, Jake stumbled up the sidewalk away from all the police cars and medical vehicles. The officer watched him for a moment. Jake faked a few gags, as if something were coming up any second. This made the officer turn away, clearly not wanting to watch someone throw up. Jake could feel his adrenaline soaring. If he had any chance at getting to his daughter, this was his moment. He had to run like hell, and right now. Planting a foot in the pavement, Jake suddenly took off down the sidewalk as fast as he possibly could.

He heard the officer shout, "Hey, wait a second!"

Jake didn't slow down. He kept running. He wondered if the guy would start shooting at him. He was only being detained and not arrested. How far would they go to stop him from getting away? He had to take that chance. At the next street corner, Jake darted to his left. He took his first peek over his shoulder. He spotted two officers running down the sidewalk after him. Then his view was blocked by the house on the street corner. He heard police sirens again. Others were likely getting into police cars to pursue him. Jake knew he needed to somehow get off the main streets and find his way into the shadows of the neighborhood. But he couldn't just secure a hiding spot and stay put. They would eventually find him. He had to keep running. The next few minutes were critical. The longer anyone had eyes on him, the more likely he'd be caught.

Jake turned down another street, pumping his legs as fast as he could. He had fortunately gotten himself back into good shape over the past few months since he'd had the free time to run and exercise without a real job. This was paying off for him now. Another peek over his shoulder. The two officers were still back there, but he was gradually losing them. Unfortunately, he couldn't outrun police cars and radios. He cut through a front yard to get to the next street, then raced down a steep hill. The slope almost caused him to face-plant on asphalt. The sirens were getting closer. Sounded like a swarm of them, coming from different directions—he couldn't be sure.

Then a police car suddenly swerved into the street directly in front of him, blinding him with bright headlights. Jake cursed, darted into someone's driveway to his right. He had to get off the grid right now, or this would be over before he even got started. The house was a two-story gray stone number with a side garage. Jake swung open a wooden gate to the backyard, hoping no one was out there grilling or something.

Barely slowing, Jake hustled through the backyard and found himself staring at a kids' playscape in the back corner. Right beyond it was a wooden fence. Jake could hear the police car skid to a stop right in front of the house. More sirens were coming up the same street. Sprinting toward the playscape, Jake bounded up the plastic slide and, without even looking, jumped over the wooden fence into someone else's backyard. He tucked before landing on his face but still came down hard on his left shoulder. He rolled clumsily a couple of times before pushing himself back up again. The house had a pool in the back. He could see lights on inside the home and a couple of kids roaming about. Hurrying around the pool, Jake found a backyard gate that led to a driveway. He flung it open, ran up the driveway, got himself back onto another main street. He'd created some momentary clearance.

Peering over to his right, Jake spotted a sign that said WALSH BOAT LANDING. He realized he was running along Lake Austin Boulevard, which butted up against the river. Cutting away from the street, he sprinted through a grassy park area and down toward a boat dock. He hopped a metal railing, caught a toe on the pavement on the other side, and took a tumble where he hit his head hard. He could now hear sirens on Lake Austin Boulevard behind him. Had they spotted him? Pushing himself back up again, he stayed low as he hurried out onto a dark and quiet boat dock. It was late. No people around. No boats currently tied up. There was no other place for him to go unless he jumped into the water. So that's exactly what he did. He sprinted down the length of the boat dock and dived headfirst into the frigid waters of Lake Austin.

He held his breath as long as possible, swimming as far away from the dock as he could, before he finally came up for air. He barely lifted his head out of the water before going right back under. He could hardly see a damn thing in the dark water, but he just kept on swimming. Another quick breath and then back under the water. He kept doing this until he thought he might pass out before taking his first full moment to catch his breath.

Lifting his head out of the water, he turned to take a glance back at the dock. He was shocked by how far from shore he'd already swum. He was halfway to the other side of Lake Austin. He could see red and blue flashing lights on the street beyond the dock and what looked like officers shining flashlights all around. One of them finally came down to the dock and started looking out over the water. Jake ducked below the water, turned, started swimming again. He waited until he thought he might drown before barely lifting his mouth, just enough to catch a breath. Then back under, away from the dock, making his way to the other side. It took him about ten more minutes before he finally found land again in the dark recesses of a swampy shoreline.

He turned around to peer back toward the dock on the other side of the water. It didn't look like any police officers were still there searching for him. He pulled himself clear of the water, feeling completely exhausted. He'd done it. He'd managed to get away. But now what? His whole body was shaking. He needed to get into dry clothes before he got hypothermia. And then he had to find and rescue Piper.

SEVEN

Dani Nolan got the call from her boss while standing in the backyard of her two-bedroom condo in her flannel pajamas, waiting for her dog, Bailey, to finally take a crap. Her golden retriever could sometimes take forever. She had to first sniff every square inch of grass. Dani was extra frustrated tonight because of the crisp chill in the air. Looking at her phone, Dani sighed, wondering if this call was going to be personal or FBI related. She really didn't have the energy for either at the moment. She just wanted to crawl up in her bed with Bailey and find something mindless to binge on Netflix until she fell asleep. It had already been a long week. She was looking forward to a much-needed day off tomorrow.

"Hey, Simon," she answered.

"Dani, we got a problem."

"We have lots of problems. That's why we're on a break, remember?"

"I'm not talking about you and me for once."

"What is it?"

"Someone in our office was shot dead a few minutes ago."

"Damn. Who?"

"Caitlin Kingston. Have you met her? She just started doing analytics work over in Martin's department. Young gal—straight out of school."

Dani repeated the name. "I don't think so. What happened?"

"I don't know. I need you to go find out."

"Seriously? I'm in my pajamas already."

"The sexy red silky ones?"

"Simon . . ."

"Look, I don't want to send Mason over there for this."

"Why? He's actually *on duty*."

"Apparently, the girl's grandfather is kind of a big deal. I want to make sure we handle this right from the beginning. I don't need any extra headaches right now. I trust you way more than I trust Mason."

"If this is your way of winning me back, it's a lousy strategy."

"I'm sorry. I really am. But I need you there ASAP."

"Fine. Text me the address."

Fifteen minutes later, Dani drove her black Mazda SUV down a narrow street already packed with police and emergency vehicles. She'd pulled her brown hair into a ponytail and put on a black ball cap because her hair was still wet from her shower earlier. After parking and getting out, she tugged on her standard dark-blue jacket with *FBI* emblazoned in yellow on the back. She'd been trying to place the girl in the office who'd been killed tonight but was having difficulty. Dani was still new herself, having moved from DC only six months ago to join the local FBI unit. She'd never expected to come back home to Austin. DC was the center of the FBI world. She'd already put in thirteen good years there, working her way up the special agent ranks. But her father had grown ill over the past year, and she didn't trust her kid brother to provide the kind of care he needed in his last days. Even at thirty-five, her brother was still a goof-off and could never seem to keep a job longer than a few months. He'd rather sit around his dumpy apartment and play video games all day.

Snaking through all the police vehicles, Dani finally stepped up in front of a white two-story modern house with police officers, medical professionals, and what was probably family all standing outside. A young uniformed officer was already making eyes at her while leaning against his car, doing nothing useful. She'd stopped being shocked a long time ago at how some guys were willing to flirt with her at crime scenes. As if they were all just hanging out at a sports bar.

"Who's in charge?" she asked the officer.

The guy nodded down the sidewalk. "Detective Kramer."

She spotted a fiftysomething man with a thick mustache in a brown sport coat talking on his cell phone and then made her way over to him. Noticing her walking up, he tilted his head with a wrinkled brow. He took another few seconds to finish his call, hung up, then glanced at the logo on her jacket.

"FBI?" he said.

"Special Agent Dani Nolan."

"Detective Roger Kramer."

"Victim worked in our office."

"Right. I was told that. Well, welcome."

"What can you tell me?"

"We got a 911 call around eight reporting a disturbance, possible gunshot, and a man spotted running away from the residence. We got here shortly thereafter and found the victim on the kitchen floor. Gunshot to the stomach. One of our officers said she was unresponsive. Minutes later, a man shows back up to the house, covered in blood, claiming to be a relative. Said he walked in on the shooting and tried to chase someone up the street."

"You believe him?"

"At first, yeah. Some question marks, especially from the family of the victim. But he seemed somewhat credible. I mean, not sure why he'd come back to the crime scene if he actually shot the girl."

"You said at first. Something change your mind?"

"Well, the guy hauled ass on us a few minutes ago."

"He ran?"

"Yep. Faked out one of our officers and just took off. We're still in pursuit of him, but he seems to have momentarily given us the slip."

"Damn. You get his name before he took off?"

"Hell, I've got his entire wallet."

He took a brown leather wallet out of his jacket pocket and handed it to Dani. She opened it to examine the driver's license and stiffened. She closely examined the man's face and couldn't believe her eyes. Jake Slater?

"Everything all right?" Kramer asked her.

She nodded, swallowed. "Yeah, he just, uh . . . It seems odd that he'd come back here, give you his ID, only to take off running on you."

"Yeah, totally bizarre. Plus, he was making claims that this guy he said was inside the house when he got here had taken his daughter."

"Are there security cameras here?"

Kramer shook his head. "No cameras. The victim had just moved in this past week. Her father said they hadn't had a chance to get a new security system up and running yet. And we haven't found anything useful as far as neighbors' cameras up and down this street." His eyes narrowed on her. "You sure you're all right? You look a little pale."

"Yeah, I'm fine," Dani lied, trying to hide the shock she was feeling. "Just a little queasy. Shouldn't have had those spicy wings tonight, you know what I'm saying?"

"I do. My stomach can't handle the hot wings anymore." He grinned. "The crazy thing is that our runner actually is a relative. He's the victim's uncle. The family says his daughter was with the victim earlier this evening."

"Do they know where his daughter is now?"

Kramer shook his head. "They're concerned. We have a search out with her name and photo. Nothing has turned up yet, but it's early."

"So it could be true? Someone else could've been here."

"I suppose. But then why the hell would he run?"

She shook her head. "Doesn't add up."

"Plus, the family says there have been major issues going on between this guy and the victim's family. The grandfather of the victim claims that our runner was angry at the victim for her role in a custody battle for his daughter earlier this year. He seems to believe the guy was capable of pulling the trigger."

Dani couldn't believe that—or maybe she just didn't want to believe it. The Jake Slater she knew, and once loved, would've never been capable of such a thing. But then, it had been fifteen years. People change. She definitely had. Still, walking up onto a crime scene to find out a man she'd once believed she'd spend the rest of her life with was a likely suspect in a murder was a total shocker. She wasn't even sure what to do with the information at the moment.

"We'll be aiding in the investigation," Dani stated. "We have to make sure this isn't connected to our office in any way."

"Of course. We could use your resources." Kramer looked beyond her and suddenly cursed. "Just great."

Dani turned, followed his eyes toward the street. A local news van had just pulled up. Two guys hopped out, one clearly the on-air talent with his perfectly sculpted hair and impeccable suit. The other guy wore camo pants and scrambled to grab camera gear from the back.

"That was fast," Dani said.

"The victim comes from a prominent local family."

"Yeah, I heard about that."

"This is going to turn into a three-ring circus real quick. You want to handle it? You'd look much better on camera. My wife says I look fat on TV."

"No, thanks. I don't play nice with the media."

"Too bad. Wish me luck."

EIGHT

Jake made a trek in the shadows along the bank of the river for over two miles before finally crossing a walking bridge to the opposite shoreline. Shivering in his wet clothes, he now stood in front of Stephen F. Austin High School, where he used to coach. The big parking lot outside the school was mostly empty. It was Saturday night. No one should be around. But the parking lot was still well lit, which left him feeling exposed. Because running across the parking lot might make him stand out even more, he walked as quickly but casually as possible, hands in jacket pockets, just some guy out for a late-night stroll—not someone the police were looking for right now. He still couldn't believe he'd somehow managed to evade them. Thankfully, he hadn't seen a police car since he'd climbed out of the water about thirty minutes ago.

As he walked, Jake pulled out his phone, which was water resistant and still seemed to be operating OK. Unfortunately, there had been no further communication between him and Piper. He had tried calling her back, thinking that even if whoever held her captive answered, Jake somehow might be able to reason with them. Maybe offer them money—*anything* for them to release her! But his calls only went straight to her voice mail. Her captors had likely turned her phone off or maybe even destroyed it entirely. Again, he tried not to think about how Piper was feeling right now: scared, vulnerable, and all alone. He just had to keep moving forward until he found her.

Jake approached a back entrance to the high school near the athletic offices and locker rooms, where he used to go in and out all the time. There was a bulletin board hung up on the brick wall outside the back door that held various school flyers and announcements. Reaching behind one corner of the board, Jake began feeling around until his fingers settled on something very familiar. He felt a wave of relief pour through him. The magnetic key box was still there. When coaching, he used to always forget his key to the school. So he'd hidden a spare back there a while ago that had repeatedly saved him.

He quickly pulled the key out, stuck it in the keyhole, slipped inside, and then pulled the metal door closed behind him. He immediately embraced the warmth of the building. Standing in the back hallway, Jake listened for a moment. He didn't expect anyone else to be inside the school. Not even the cleaning crew, since kids weren't around on the weekends. At least, that was his hope. Still, he wanted to get in and out as quickly as possible.

The football offices, locker rooms, and weight room were just around the corner from the back door. Jake hustled forward, paused to take a quick peek into the next hallway, and then turned the corner. Most of the lights were off in the building, but he could still easily make his way around. He opened another door to the football wing, stepped into his old stomping grounds, and turned on a light switch. Multiple coaches' offices lined both sides of the hallway. At the back of the hallway was the coaches' locker room. Jake headed straight for it, eager to strip out of his wet clothes. Once inside, he started searching locker cubbies for any clothes that might fit him. Coaches always had something around. He was quickly able to pull together a full wardrobe—a pair of black jogging pants, a gray T-shirt, a maroon hoodie, boxers, socks, and even a pair of running shoes that ran just slightly big on him. Peeling out of his wet clothes, he put on his dry wardrobe and felt his whole body begin to slowly thaw.

Jake walked into the adjacent bathroom near the coaches' showers, hit the light switch, and then stood over a sink in front of a mirror. He looked beat to hell. Examining his face, he noticed a big scrape under his left chin and a small gash at the top of his forehead from his various tumbles. It reminded him of the way he'd looked when he'd woken up in the hospital after the car crash last year.

Jake grabbed a small mirror that was sitting on the hospital table next to his bed and held it up to his face. A white bandage covered his forehead. His bottom lip was busted. There was a gash on his cheek. A doctor he recognized from earlier came into the room. Jake didn't care about how he looked right now. He only cared about his family.

"Piper?" Jake asked the doctor.

"Some broken bones, but she's going to be OK."

Relief poured through him. "Sarah?"

The grim expression on the doctor's face said everything. "I'm sorry, Mr. Slater."

Jake's first thought was his daughter. "Does Piper know?"

The doctor shook his head. "We thought you might want to be there."

Jake ignored the doctor's insistence on a wheelchair and limped down the hallway to his daughter's hospital room. She looked tiny in the bed, like she was six years old. Her eyes were closed. A white bandage covered half her face. A nurse was messing with a machine but left when Jake sidled up next to the bed. He wanted to scoop up his baby and hold her close to him, but he knew he couldn't do that right now. Her body was broken. And within minutes, her heart would be shattered, too. He leaned over her, which caused her eyes to flutter open. She blinked several times, and then she was aware of him.

"Daddy!"

She reached for him. He held her gently, tears pouring down his cheeks. He tried to fight them off—he wanted to be strong for her right now—but he couldn't help it. Her world was about to be rocked. Jake knew the feeling. His mother had died in a car accident when he was only ten. He'd never forget the moment his dad came into his bedroom and shared the news with him, like a brand permanently burned into his chest. It devastated him to put that same brand into his daughter right now.

"Where's Mommy?" Piper asked.

Jake swallowed. There was no way to cloak this news. He just had to be honest with her. "She's gone, baby. Mom is gone."

The sound his daughter made next frightened him. He'd never heard an audible gasp quite like that before. Then tears. Then fighting for breath. Jake held her trembling body in his arms, rocking her gently.

"I'm here, baby. I'm here." He just kept repeating it over and over again. "We're going to be OK. I promise. I'm here. You and me. Always."

Turning on the hot water, Jake splashed his face and tried to get himself cleaned up. He noticed that his hands were still really shaking. But it was no longer from being cold. It was the absolute shock of his new reality. Piper had been taken. Her life was in danger. Caitlin had been shot and killed. His niece was dead. And he was on the run from the police. It was impossible to wrap his mind around it all. Because he'd fled, Jake figured his involvement was no longer in doubt by the police. Unless they'd discovered contrary evidence—which he prayed they did—the police most certainly now viewed him as a primary suspect. But it would all be worth it if he got Piper back tonight.

Jake took several deep breaths and let them out slowly. He had to stay calm and focused. Continuing to freak out was going to get him nowhere fast—it certainly wasn't going to help him find Piper. He needed to think as clearly as possible. He stuffed his wet clothes and jacket in the bottom of an oversize trash can. Then he hurried back into the football offices and sat down inside his old head coach's office, which had now been taken over by his best friend and former assistant coach, Drew Beamer. He wiggled the mouse on the desktop, watched the computer screen come to life. He would need a password to access the system. Drew was a simple guy. Jake doubted he had a password that was too complicated. First he typed in Drew's wife's name: *Maggie*. Denied. He then tried his son's name: *Zach*. Denied. Jake racked his brain. Drew had gone to college with him back at Sam Houston State and played tight end on the team. Jake typed in *Bearkats*, the school mascot. Bingo. Access granted.

Pulling up Google on the desktop, Jake typed *Judd McGee* and *Address*, hoping to find a quick answer to where Judd lived. But nothing obvious popped up. He tried different versions of the same search but still came up empty-handed. The man's address was not listed anywhere. How was he going to find it? He then typed in *Judd McGee* and the name *Beth*. That didn't pull up anything, either. He exited out of Google and began searching the desktop screen for other folders that might have student contact information. He knew they had something like that on the school server. Jake searched through a dozen different screen folders but couldn't locate anything like it.

Frustrated, he pushed back from the desk and ran his fingers through his hair. His eyes drifted over to one of Drew's family photos sitting up on the desk. Maybe his old pal could help him. Jake knew from monitoring his former football team from a distance that Drew had allowed Judd's son, Quinn, to come back and play this year. They were winning again. It had kind of pissed him off after all the grief Jake had put himself through last year—which was why he and Drew hadn't talked in several months.

That, and it was just too damn hard. Coaching had been his life. And he'd lost it.

Jake took out his cell phone and typed a text to Drew.

Hey, bud. What're you doing?

He waited to see if he'd get a quick response. He did.

Drew: Just got through watching the Horns hammer Auburn at DKR. Down on Sixth Street right now with some friends watching other games. You?

DKR was short for Darrell K. Royal Memorial Stadium, where the University of Texas football team played their home games. Jake knew the Longhorns had a big game against the Auburn Tigers today. He'd watched a little of it while in his hotel room this afternoon. Sixth Street, Austin's famous party district, would likely be packed to the rim in the aftermath of a home game. It wasn't too far away from the high school, and the massive crowds might make it a safe place to meet. Should he risk it? On one hand, it seemed foolish to expose himself anywhere right now. However, he hoped to be able to get more than just info about Judd McGee from Drew. Jake needed cash. The police had taken his wallet. He wasn't going to get very far with no money at all. Still, he didn't want to walk straight into a crowded bar without some sort of disguise. And he also needed a vehicle. He couldn't travel everywhere on foot.

Thankfully, Jake had ideas to solve both issues.

He quickly followed up with another text.

Can we meet up ASAP?

Drew: You in town?

Yes, it's important.

Drew: Of course, man! Been way too long. Just tell me when and where.

Meet me at BBG's on Sixth in 20 minutes.

NINE

Dani called in a small crew of other FBI agents to work the crime scene with her. While she couldn't wrap her mind around the possibility that Jake Slater had shot and killed his own niece tonight, she still had a job to do. Dani couldn't allow her personal connection to this situation to cloud her professional judgment. Admittedly, she probably should have immediately told Simon, her boss, and recused herself from the investigation, but something kept stopping her from doing that—or even telling *anyone*. She'd heard police orders go out to find and secure the suspect by *whatever means necessary*. Dani knew exactly what that meant, and she didn't like the thought of Jake being shot out there before she even had a chance to get the full truth from him.

Dani started with the victim's family. After interviewing different members, she felt it was clear that at least a couple of them believed Jake could've done such a thing. Especially Jake's former father-in-law, Lars Kingston, the powerful patriarch of the family whom Simon had warned her about. According to Lars, Jake had been reckless, out of control, and vindictive for most of the past year. Jake wanted to hurt their family. Lars demanded she find him as soon as possible and bring him to justice. Lars seemed more angry than upset, but it was probably just his way of dealing with the grief of losing his granddaughter, Caitlin. Powerful men did not like to feel powerless.

One of the victim's uncles claimed that Caitlin Kingston had told him how angry Jake had been during a phone call a few months ago. The uncle said Jake didn't feel like Caitlin had supported him enough during a tough custody battle over Piper. While the uncle never suspected it would go this far, he also felt like Jake was a bit of a loose cannon. None of the family knew where Jake's daughter, Piper, was at the moment. They had been repeatedly trying to call her, but with no response. Interviewing this family tonight felt surreal, considering it was one of their own who had swooped in fifteen years ago and stolen the man she'd loved. Dani and Jake had their whole future mapped out. He was an up-and-coming young coach, and she was finishing up her graduate degree in criminal justice. She had been expecting a proposal at any moment. They had talked about it for a few months. And then Sarah Kingston had shown up out of nowhere with all her glitz and glamour and wrecked everything. At least, that's what Dani always believed. Jake had tried to insist it was only about his career, but Dani never bought it—especially when she found out they'd become engaged only nine months after his and Dani's breakup.

Dani had moved to DC to start a new life—something she thought she'd be doing with Jake. She'd married a lawyer named Craig, but they'd lasted only six tough years. Craig had wanted a family. They'd tried for four years before the pain of not being able to get pregnant became too much for both of them. Dani threw herself into her work. Craig eventually threw himself into another woman's bed. Her ex was now married to that woman, and they had two young kids.

Dani knew about Jake tragically losing Sarah in the car accident last year because of shared social media friends. She'd considered reaching out to him a few times when she'd moved back to town earlier this year—just to see how he was doing—but she never did. There was still some lingering pain there, even though what had happened between them was a lifetime ago.

A twentysomething agent named Eric Mitchell walked over to her. He was wearing the same FBI jacket as Dani and the others. She liked Mitchell. Fresh out of the academy, he was raw but eager to learn. She appreciated that about him. So many of the other agents were so cocky, it was near impossible to teach them anything worthwhile. Of course, she probably had the same attitude back in the day. But not Mitchell, which was why she always requested him on her cases.

"We've got a hit," Mitchell said, eyes flashing, looking at his phone.

"Suspect's phone signal?"

"Yep. Tracking it right now."

"Where?"

Mitchell showed her a digital map on the screen. "It's popping up a few miles from here, over in downtown proper. Signal is on the move."

"What about the phone of the suspect's daughter?"

He shook his head. "Nothing. Dead end."

"OK, gather the others. Let's get going."

"You want me to say something to the detective?"

Dani considered it for a moment. She should probably say yes but couldn't do it. "No, we'll bring him in ourselves. They'll just clumsy it up."

"Copy that."

Watching Mitchell hurry off to rally the others, Dani stood there a moment and silently berated herself. Clouded judgment, indeed. While she did believe getting the police involved in Jake's apprehension would only make things more complicated—after all, they'd just mucked it up here—she certainly had ulterior motives. Dani wanted to be the first one to speak to him. She felt certain she would know the truth just by looking him square in the eyes. Jake had never been able to lie to her.

TEN

Jake was innocent in Caitlin's death. But he was now guilty of a growing list of lesser crimes in the aftermath. Evading police. Breaking and entering. And he'd just added car theft. The beat-up white Ford truck was branded on the side with *AISD Maintenance*. Jake was friends with Javier, the head of the high school's maintenance department. The white school truck was always parked next to two maintenance sheds inside a secured fenced-in utility area attached to the school. Jake had borrowed the truck from Javier countless times over the years to haul around larger football gear. The truck's key was in the same place as always—hanging from a lanyard on a hook on the wall behind Javier's desk. Jake figured no one would even realize the truck was missing until first thing on Monday morning. Thankfully, the gas tank was nearly full.

After parking on a side street downtown, Jake stood at the corner of Sixth Street and Congress and took in the massive party crowd in front of him. Sixth Street was a five-block entertainment district lined with every bar, club, and music venue imaginable. Although Jake had frequented it often in his younger, unmarried days, he hadn't spent too much time down here in recent years. He slung a black backpack he'd found at the high school over his right shoulder. It was stuffed with various clothes and costume items he'd pilfered from the high school's drama department—more theft. He had no idea what he might be encountering out here but felt better equipped to deal with it now. He was currently wearing a brown knit ski cap pulled down low on his head, covering every strand of his wavy brown hair, along with fake black square-rimmed glasses. It was surreal to be dressing up in some kind of stupid costume. But what choice did he have? He didn't want anyone recognizing him right now.

Pushing off the building, Jake made his way toward the crowd. He knew police would be up and down Sixth Street. He'd already spotted two of them across the way on the opposite sidewalk, dealing with an overly raucous group. He was second-guessing his decision to come here. But he decided not to turn back, considering he was only two minutes away from meeting with Drew and hopefully getting the critical info and cash he needed. As he crossed in front of the historic Driskill hotel, Jake entered the crowd. It was like walking into a cornfield and immediately being engulfed on all sides. He pushed his way through the people, most of whom seemed highly intoxicated. A majority of them wore burnt-orange Texas Longhorn gear, but there were also pockets of Auburn Tigers fans sprinkled throughout. Everyone was partying, regardless of who won today.

Jake finally made his way up to the entrance of BBG's sports bar, which sat in the middle of a strip of other bars. He paused for a moment and scanned the crowd inside. There was a long bar top on the right side and tables lining the other side. Nearly every chair was taken. There were probably fifty large TVs stuck on every bit of wall space available, showing various college football games and other sports. It took Jake a moment to find Drew sitting by himself near the back of the room at the end of the bar. Drew was a big man at six four and probably 250 pounds with a thick beard. He wore a maroon Austin High ball cap and a gray sweatshirt. It was strange to think of him as the head football coach when the man had been Jake's top assistant for more than a decade.

A year ago, Jake had returned to his head-coaching duties only a week after Sarah's death, against his doctor's recommendation. He had been climbing the walls sitting around and just being sad all day. It was a stupid decision. Especially because he had also started drinking more heavily to help numb the pain. His team was riding a seven-game losing streak into the final game of the year but had found themselves up by three points late in the game against their rival. It was intense. Jake had been all over one referee the whole night whom he felt had made several calls going against them.

Then it happened. One of the opposing team's players clearly held one his guys right in front of the same ref and made the way for a go-ahead touchdown. Jake was irate and, truthfully, a little drunk. He let the referee have it with some descriptive words as they jawed at each other up close and personal. Then the referee leaned in and said, "Sober up, coach. Don't let your dead wife ruin my night, too." Without realizing what he was doing, Jake had his right hand wrapped around the ref's neck, squeezing with all his strength, before Drew had pulled him away. He was fired the next day. Jake might've been terminated regardless, but that incident had made it much easier for the school to get rid of a head coach who had just tragically lost his wife.

Taking one more glance behind him, checking for police and not finding any around, Jake stepped fully into BBG's. He weaved through the crowd until he made his way back to Drew and then slid onto a stool next to his friend.

Drew turned, said, "Sorry, pal, this one is taken."

Jake looked over at him. "Hey, man, it's me."

Drew cocked his head. "Dude, what's with the glasses and ski cap?"

"Long story."

They shared a quick bro hug.

"It's really good to see you," Drew said. "Even if you do look like a weirdo."

"Same. Listen, I don't have much time."

Drew's forehead bunched. "Everything OK?"

"No. I can't explain right now. But I need your help."

"Of course, man. What's going on?"

"I need to find Judd McGee ASAP."

This seemed to catch Drew off guard. "Why?"

"Like I said, long story. But it's important to me. Do you know where he lives? Or have a way of finding his address for me?"

"I can probably pull it up from the school server on my phone."

"I need you to do that for me."

"What's going on, Jake?"

"I don't have time to explain. I'm sorry. I just need this *right now*."

"All right, all right." Drew typed on his phone screen and a minute later had found an address listed on a player contact list. Jake borrowed a pen from the bartender, wrote it down on a napkin, and stuffed it in his pocket.

"His son is back on the team, you know," Drew mentioned. "I felt like he deserved another chance."

"I know. It's fine. I don't care."

"Really? Because I figured that might be why you stopped responding to my calls and texts."

"No, it's OK. You did what you had to do. Let me ask you something. Does Judd ever drive a tow truck?"

Drew shrugged. "No idea."

"He still work at an auto shop?"

"I think so. Seriously, Jake, what is this all about?"

Jake considered whether he should say anything more to Drew. After all, the man was his best friend. Maybe his only friend left. Drew was one of the few guys who had stood by him in the days that followed his firing last year. He actually told Jake that he wouldn't take over the head coaching job at Austin High if Jake didn't want him to do it. Of course, Jake insisted he take it.

Jake's eyes drifted over to a TV on the wall behind the bar to his left—one of the few that didn't have sports on it. Instead, it was tuned to a local cable news station. Jake cursed, his eyes widening. An up-close photo of him during his coaching days was currently plastered on the TV. Although Jake couldn't hear anything, the TV had closed captioning, so he could see the words scrolling across the bottom. *Jake Slater . . . suspect in death of a twenty-two-year-old woman . . . former disgraced coach of Austin High . . . Police are searching . . . The FBI is also involved.*

The TV screen switched to a male reporter at the scene of the crime. Jake immediately recognized Caitlin's house behind him. Seeing his own face and name appear on TV felt like a body blow that took the breath right out of him. He looked over at his friend. Drew was also staring at the TV. Then his buddy looked back to Jake with his mouth dropped open.

"Jake, what the hell?"

"It's not true," Jake insisted. "You have to believe me."

"Uh, OK. But what . . . ?"

"I've got to get out of here."

"Wait, Jake. What the hell am I supposed to do about this?"

Jake reached down to the floor, grabbed his backpack. "Nothing."

"Nothing? If it's not true, then let me help you."

"All right. If you want to help, I need cash. Whatever you have on you."

Drew reached into his blue jeans pocket and pulled out a wad of cash. "Take it. Probably two hundred bucks or so. It's yours."

"Thanks." Jake grabbed it, shoved it into his pocket. "I'll be in touch."

Spinning around, Jake began to make his way back to the front of the bar near the sidewalk. Then he froze in his tracks. He spotted two men up ahead of him standing in the entrance of BBG's, both wearing similar dark-blue windbreakers. The men were clearly not barhopping. Both were shoving their phones in front of people. Squinting, Jake thought they were sharing the same photo of him the news had just flashed up on the TV screen. FBI? But how would they know he was inside this bar? How the hell had they found him so fast?

Then one of the men turned and put his eyes directly on Jake.

ELEVEN

Jake spun around, hoping the guy in the dark windbreaker hadn't recognized him because of his ski cap and glasses, and began to quickly move toward the back of the bar again. His heart was hammering in his chest. If the guy still had eyes on him, where would Jake go? He peered up ahead. It looked like his only option was to hit the kitchen and try to find a back door into the alley behind the strip of buildings. He slipped through a big group of people standing around a table. As he did, Jake cast a quick look over his shoulder and cursed again. Both of the men in windbreakers were fully locked in on him and now making their way through the crowd in his direction. They knew it was him. It was no longer time for Jake to be casual about this—it was time to run like hell.

Jake bolted for the kitchen. Pushing through a swivel door, he nearly collided with a waitress coming from the other direction with a tray full of food. Jake swerved, ducked under the tray, lost his footing, and then slid on the slick kitchen floor into a wall with a crash. Everyone in the hot and loud kitchen turned to stare at the unexpected interruption. Jake pushed himself up, his eyes searching in all directions, looking for the exit. He spotted a hallway over to his right and scrambled for it. Inside the hallway, Jake reached up and pulled down a large row of metal shelves behind him. Various dishes and boxes crashed down everywhere. He hoped it would buy him precious extra seconds. He could now hear shouting going on back in the kitchen. A man clearly yelled out, *"FBI!"*

Pushing through the back door, Jake stumbled out into a dark alley. There were several dirty metal dumpsters directly in front of him, pressed up against an adjacent brick building that was connected to a multilevel parking garage. Jake wondered if there was some way to block the back door to the bar but couldn't find anything to do the trick. Because BBG's was in the middle of the strip of buildings, Jake had about the same distance to make it to either side street. He chose left and took off running again. But he got only a few feet in that direction before a man in a similar windbreaker appeared in the alley up ahead of him. Jake skidded to a sudden stop when he saw the man reach down to his side and pull something out. Was it a gun? He wasn't going to get close enough to find that out. Pivoting, Jake took off in the opposite direction.

As he passed by the back door of BBG's again, he heard it swing open behind him. The other two guys were going to be close on his heels now. Jake was about fifty feet from the next side street when yet another person appeared. Same dark windbreaker. But this was a woman. And not just any woman. Jake stopped, stared, completely stunned. *Dani?*

He knew her face so well, even if it had aged slightly. He would still dream about her sometimes and had often wondered how life might have turned out if he'd chosen differently. But seeing Dani standing there in front of him in this moment with a gun held at her side was surreal. Jake felt trapped. But he noticed she never raised her gun. He looked over to his left, where the parking garage butted up against the adjacent building. Entry into the parking garage from the alley was completely blocked by chain-link fencing. Jake spotted one corner of the fence that had been peeled back.

Without thinking twice, he rushed over to the fence, dropped to his knees, and began to squeeze his way headfirst through the tight opening. He could feel the metal wiring scrape down his entire body as he wriggled himself all the way through. A second later, Jake was into the parking-garage level. He hit the floor in a full sprint. The FBI agents were yelling at him to stop. Not wanting to give them the chance to shoot, Jake ducked behind a row of parked cars, kept his head low, and basically crab-walked as fast as he could toward an exit on the opposite side of the garage. He knew one thing for sure. Like earlier when he'd run, he couldn't stay out in the open for long. There was no way for him to outrun radio signals—especially when dealing with the FBI. They might already have a drone or something else flying overhead.

Rushing out of the parking garage, Jake found his way onto another sidewalk. While the bigger crowds were back on Sixth Street, there were still plenty of people meandering about on Seventh and making their way in that direction. Jake darted to his left, trying not to run so fast that he drew suspicious looks, searching everywhere for a way to disappear. He spotted a taxi parked on the curb up ahead of him. He considered it for a moment but didn't trust that the driver would adequately speed away. Jake couldn't risk that. Still, he had to do something quick. The FBI agents would be on him any second.

Cutting across the street, Jake hopped up onto the opposite sidewalk and hustled toward another alley. For now, he would just keep running, alley to alley, staying in the city shadows as much as possible. He was surprised he did not hear police sirens nearby. Was the FBI acting alone? Jake found his way onto Eighth Street and was about to duck into yet another dark alley when he noticed something up ahead of him. Part of the sidewalk was sectioned off by construction barriers. A truck labeled *City of Austin Watershed Protection Department* was parked on the curb right next to the barriers. It looked like there was an open manhole in the sidewalk. There were no workers standing around. Jake thought he spotted a guy inside the truck, talking on the phone.

This would certainly be off the grid. But where the hell would the city's underground drainage system take him?

There was only one way to find out. Jake slipped around the barriers and then carefully crawled down the manhole on a steel ladder before finally setting foot onto wet concrete inside a drainage tunnel about five feet deep. Pulling his phone out, he turned on the flashlight. He stood in a couple of inches of brown water that looked to be moving to his left. Using his phone to guide him, Jake followed the water's path while staying hunched over the entire time to keep from banging his head up against the ceiling of the tunnel. He tried not to think about how claustrophobic he suddenly felt while being trapped inside this tunnel. Instead, he focused on getting to Piper. That kept his feet moving forward.

Every fifty yards or so, he would come upon the underside of another manhole cover. He pushed up on one, just to see if he could lift it off. The covers were incredibly heavy but not impossible to slide away. That made him feel less trapped. He also began intersecting with a lot of connecting tunnels. Whenever he was at a crossroads, he decided to keep following the flow of water with the thought that it was likely taking him south toward the river. The farther he went, the safer he felt, until he eventually found himself at the very end of a tunnel looking out over the part of the Colorado River known as Lady Bird Lake. He again thought about Dani, still stunned about coming face-to-face with her. He hadn't seen her up close and personal since the day they'd broken up fifteen years ago.

"I can't do this," Jake said.

Dani was sitting on the park bench. He was standing and sweating. He'd been dreading this moment all day. But he knew it was right. He was a Texas high school football coach. He always would be—it was in his blood. He couldn't move to DC with Dani. He'd thought he could do it—which was why they'd started talking about getting married a couple of months ago. He regretted that now. It made this so much harder. She had to go. But he had to stay.

"Do what?" Dani said.

"I can't go with you."

The shock was clear on Dani's face. "But . . . you said . . ."

"I know. I'm so sorry."

"I don't understand."

"It's complicated. I just—"

Jake watched as her brow tightened up. "It's her, isn't it?"

"Who?"

"Sarah Kingston."

"No, she's just a friend, Dani. I told you that. Nothing else."

He wasn't lying. Sarah was just a friend.

"Does she know that, Jake? Because I can see it all over her when she's around you."

"Dani . . . it's nothing. This is not about her."

She was quickly getting angry. "I should've known. I never trusted her."

"Dani, please."

Tears hit her eyes. But Dani was tough. She didn't want him to see them. He reached for her. She forcefully knocked his hand away. This was not how he wanted this to go down.

"Don't touch me!"

She stood, ready to bolt.

"Wait," Jake pleaded. "Can we talk about this?"

"What's to talk about? You've clearly already made up your mind."

Thinking back to that moment, Jake shook his head. Dani never responded to any of his texts or calls after that difficult conversation. Crawling out of the tunnel, Jake sloshed through ankle-deep water, then climbed back onto dry land next to a running trail near the Congress

Avenue Bridge. He felt relieved to stretch out his back. Taking a moment to get his bearings, Jake again wondered how the FBI had found him so quickly. Could Drew have told them about their meeting after he'd first texted? Would his friend actually do that? But then how would the FBI have even known about Drew? It seemed unlikely they could have anticipated Jake reaching out to this particular friend in such a short amount of time. And Drew clearly had no idea about his current predicament when he'd first sat down at the bar.

Jake noticed the flashlight was still engaged on his phone and pressed a button to turn it off. Staring at his phone, he suddenly cursed as it dawned on him. His phone. The FBI had tracked him on his damn phone. He cursed again. He hadn't even considered that possibility. That was stupid. He had to turn it off. Or better yet, get rid of it. But then how would Piper get ahold of him should she somehow get the chance to reach out again? Still, Jake couldn't risk it. If the FBI had tracked his phone to the bar, then they were probably tracking him down right now and might be here at any second. Jake took a moment to study Piper's new phone number, committing it to memory. Then he reared back and tossed his phone as far as he could out into the river. He turned and began sprinting down the running trail in the opposite direction.

TWELVE

Dani stood under the Congress Avenue Bridge and stared out over the calm, dark waters of Lady Bird Lake. Her breath was still short from all the running. Standing next to her, Agent Mitchell studied a digital map on his phone screen. The rest of her FBI team was out on the running trail on both sides in search of Jake, whom they'd lost track of just a few minutes ago. Dani was shocked by how Jake had managed to think so quickly on his feet by choosing to use the city's drainage tunnels to evade them. It had taken them too long to realize how he'd suddenly disappeared, and that had cost them dearly. Jake was gone—for now.

"It's in the water, Dani," Mitchell said. "I'm certain of it."

She sighed. "He must've realized we were tracking his phone."

"Yeah, that, or the man is a mermaid who can hold his breath for a long damn time. Because the signal is just sitting out there stationary, right in front of us."

She gave a half smile, reflecting. "Jake's a good swimmer but not *that* good."

Mitchell tilted his head at her. "What?"

Realizing what she'd just said, Dani quickly dismissed it. "Nothing. Just . . . nothing. Let's get someone down here ASAP to retrieve the phone."

"Copy that."

"And let's get back over to the bar. I want to know what that guy was doing in there. Seems odd he put himself in those crowds for some reason."

Dani emphasized *that guy* since she'd foolishly used Jake's first name a second ago. She was walking an ethical tightrope and wondered if this would all backfire on her eventually. She didn't need to be risking her job for an old flame she hadn't even talked to in fifteen years.

She thought back to roughly twenty minutes ago, when she and Jake had stared right at each other in the dark alley. Had Jake recognized her? There was a split second when she thought she saw a hint of recognition cross his face. Did Jake know she was back in Austin? Had he been keeping up with her through social media like she had with him the past decade? Had Jake thought about her at all over the years? She cursed, shook her head, realizing that last question had nothing at all to do with this case. But she couldn't deny how seeing him up close and personal had unexpectedly made her feel. And that was already complicating this investigation for her.

After all, she couldn't even get herself to raise her own damn gun.

THIRTEEN

After retrieving his stolen truck from downtown, Jake drove to South Austin and settled in the corner of a half-full parking lot in front of a Walmart Supercenter. He didn't think the store closed until 11:00 p.m. Before getting out, he rummaged through his newfound black backpack and pulled out a blue baseball cap with an American flag on the front and a dark-gray zip-up cotton jacket. He'd already packed away the ski cap and fake square-rimmed glasses—the FBI had just seen him in those. It was probably smart for him to keep mixing up his look from this point forward. He then pulled out a small black kit from inside the backpack and opened it. It was a costume kit with all types of fake facial hair. Mustaches, beards, goatees, the works. He had worked with fake facial hair once before in high school, when he was an extra in the play *Van Helsing*. This wasn't completely foreign territory for him.

Jake selected a simple brown mustache and then grabbed a small bottle of spirit gum along with an applicator brush. Opening the bottle, he dipped in the small brush and then rubbed the clear liquid on his upper lip while staring at himself in the rearview mirror. The bottle instructed him to let it sit for a few seconds to get tacky. Then he carefully placed the fake mustache on his upper lip and held it in place for thirty seconds. Letting go, he moved his mouth all around.

The mustache stayed in place. Studying himself, he shook his head. *Ridiculous.* But he didn't care as long as he didn't look like the same guy the FBI had just chased. Whatever the hell it took to get his daughter back.

He put on the gray jacket, pulled the ball cap down low on his forehead, and then got out of the vehicle. Hands in his pockets, Jake kept his head on a swivel as he quickly made his way up to the massive retail store. He walked through the automatic glass doors and then paused for a moment to look around for the electronics department. He spotted it over to his left. He also noted a portly security guard. The guard's eyes were set directly on Jake at the moment, which was unnerving. Would a retail-store security guard know about him already? Would the police blast out an alert about him to every avenue possible? Playing it cool, he gave the guard a courteous nod and got to moving again.

Jake had to pass through an expansive TV department to get to where he was headed. All the TVs were showcasing their vivid high-resolution screens by playing various sports and movies. But several of them were tuned to local stations. It was exactly ten o'clock. Jake paused a moment to watch as different ten o'clock news teams began their nightly broadcasts. He cursed under his breath when discovering he was the lead story on every single one of the local stations. *Jake Slater . . . suspect in death . . . police are searching . . . dangerous . . . still at large.*

Then he suddenly saw Piper's photo pop up on several of the TV screens. It was a school photo from a year ago. *Police are also searching . . . missing child . . . thirteen-year-old Piper Slater.*

It was an out-of-body experience for him to watch this all unfold on the various TV screens. Would the media publicly mentioning Piper put her in more danger? How would the people who held her captive react? He took a quick peek around him in the store. A couple of other shoppers had also stopped to watch the broadcasts. When one of them glanced over in his direction, Jake turned away and hurried off. He had to get moving even faster.

He found the section for cell phones and quickly searched the aisles until he located prepaid cell phone options. Grabbing a burner phone with internet included that he could afford with Drew's cash, Jake hustled back to the front of the store. He found the shortest checkout line available and waited. He felt very uncomfortable at the moment—like a spotlight was shining down on him. He wanted to get out of this store as soon as possible, but the woman checking out in front of him was taking her sweet time unloading her basket.

"Coach Slater?"

Jake turned, startled. A young man of probably nineteen in jeans and a black hoodie stood behind him. Jake immediately recognized him. Ben Curtis. The boy had been on his football team a few years ago. Jake swallowed, felt his chest tighten. Ben had recognized him even with the fake mustache. That was unsettling. But the casual look on the boy's face told him the kid had not yet seen the news and knew nothing about his current predicament. Still, had anyone else around them heard the boy use his name? Jake tried to stay calm, but his heart was racing. This was the last thing he needed right now.

"Hey, Ben, how're you doing?"

"Good, Coach. Working for my dad part-time while I take classes at ACC."

"Your dad is a good man. Tell him hi for me."

Jake could feel the nerves in his voice. He needed to get the hell out of there. The woman in front of him was finally finished, so Jake scooted forward and set the burner phone down in front of the cashier. He turned his back fully to the boy, hoping Ben would take the hint. But the kid didn't.

"How're you doing, Coach?" Ben asked. "I was real sorry to hear about everything that, you know, happened last year."

Jake barely turned. "Doing just fine, son. Thanks."

The cashier was going in slow motion. She clearly hated her job and was not motivated to make things quick. Jake noticed the boy looking down at the item he was purchasing with cash. Ben's face kind of bunched. Jake didn't want to get into that conversation—or any more conversation for that matter. As soon as he got his change back from the cashier, Jake was ready to bolt.

"Take care, Ben. Good to see you."

Jake didn't even wait for a reply. He headed straight for the exit. He again felt the security guard's eyes on him as he walked out. Even though it was cold, Jake was sweating up a storm underneath his cotton jacket. He was already walking quickly, but the farther he got away from the store, the faster he went—until he found himself running back to his truck. He wanted to get out of the parking lot as soon as possible in case his former player came out looking to have a longer talk with him. Plus, he didn't want Ben to see that he was driving the stolen school truck. It would only raise more questions.

Climbing inside the truck, Jake started it right up, shifted into gear, and pressed down on the gas. The truck jerked forward. Staring back at the store, he noticed Ben step outside and kind of look around. Jake slouched way down in his seat just to be safe and then drove out of the parking lot.

FOURTEEN

Once clear of Walmart, Jake pulled off into another parking lot nearby and tore open the prepaid phone package. He powered up the phone, said a quick prayer, and then called Piper's phone number. His heart sank when the call went straight to her voice mail. Was her phone temporarily off? Or had her captors destroyed it? Hearing his daughter's sweet voice mail greeting immediately brought tears to his eyes. He had listened to her record it just this morning. *Hi, this is Piper. Leave me a message, and if you're nice enough, maybe I'll call you back.* She had a cute little giggle at the end. That giggle was everything to him. Innocent. Joyful. He cherished it because there hadn't been much giggling this past year. Instead, there had been so many heavy conversations. Beginning with the first time they'd sat down together after Sarah's death to talk about somehow moving forward.

"*Who's going to help me with, you know, women's stuff?*" *Piper asked him.*

Jake stared at his daughter across the restaurant table. They were at Torchy's Tacos. It was one of their go-to father-daughter eating establishments. They both loved the spicy queso. But Piper wasn't touching it tonight. She hadn't been eating much since the funeral a week ago. She mostly just sat and stared at her food. Jake hadn't pushed her. He was not eating much, either. But he'd been drinking too much. He knew he needed to cut back, but he kept reaching for the bottle. He hadn't been able to sleep without it.

"I'll do my best," Jake said.

This was their first real talk about the future. To this point, they'd both just been walking around kind of numb all the time.

Piper rolled her eyes. "But you don't know anything about periods and girl stuff like that, Dad."

"I know a few things. And I can always go to YouTube."

It was a joke. He forced a smile. But she didn't receive it and just shook her head.

"You still have your aunts around," he mentioned. "Or you can always call Caitlin."

"I guess, it's just . . ." Tears hit her eyes. "I miss her so much."

"I know. Me too."

"I don't know what I'm going to do without her."

"You're going to be OK," he assured her.

"You promise?"

"Yes," he lied. He was not sure of anything right now. "Just going to take some time."

Jake had to fight hard to not break down right there in the parking lot. But he couldn't resist the urge to think about how scared his daughter must be. What had these people done to her? Had they hurt her? Was his little girl tied up, gagged, and every other unimaginable thing he could think of at the moment?

Steadying himself, Jake typed out a text message.

Sweetie, I love you so much! This is my new number. Call me if you get your phone back. —Dad

If you have my daughter and are reading this, please don't hurt her. I'm begging you. I will give you everything I have for her safe release. Or you can take me instead. Please call me! We can work this out! I promise!

Jake hit "Send" and said another prayer. The thought of Piper not being able to reach him if somehow given the opportunity was too much for him to bear. He had to offer some kind of communication lifeline, even if it was to her captors. He was trying to think of every possible way to resolve all this as quickly as possible.

Sitting there, Jake again thought back to about a half hour ago, when he'd encountered Dani in the alley behind the bar on Sixth Street. Using his new phone, Jake did a quick search for Dani online. He found a Facebook account that belonged to her. She now lived in Austin. There were various photos of Dani out and about with her friends around the city. There was no mention of her being remarried. He knew she had gotten married and divorced while living in DC. She'd aged well and was still every bit as attractive as she'd been in her twenties. He was not surprised. Dani always took great care of herself.

It felt surreal that a woman whom he'd once planned to marry was now actively hunting him down as part of the FBI. Could Dani possibly believe he had killed someone? Could she really suspect he was on the run because he was guilty? She had not raised her gun at him when given the chance. Why? Jake wondered if there could be any way that Dani might be willing to help him. But what was he going to do? Send her a Facebook message? A message like that would likely be traced to his new burner phone and put him right back into serious jeopardy again. He dismissed the idea.

Reaching into his pocket, Jake pulled out the bar napkin where he'd scribbled down Judd McGee's home address. He typed it into a maps app on his phone. A pin hit the map about seven miles south from where he was parked near an eclectic community of old and new called Oak Hill. Putting the truck back into gear, Jake headed in that direction. As he drove, he kept staring down at his phone, hoping to see a reply from Piper. But nothing happened. It was a Hail Mary, and he knew it.

Within ten minutes, Jake found himself driving into a middle-class neighborhood of one-story brick homes that were all likely built thirty-plus years ago. Most of them kind of sagged in various ways. He navigated the streets until he got toward the back of the subdivision. The closer he got to the pin on his phone map, the faster his heart began to race. A mix of hope and fear. All the houses sat side by side on tiny lots. If Piper was still being held inside a barn, she wasn't here—and that was disconcerting. Jake finally pulled to the curb a half block away from a white brick number with a familiar-looking pickup truck parked in the short driveway. He recognized it as the same one Judd used to drive last year. He was in the right place. He searched up and down the street but did not spot a black tow truck anywhere.

Sitting there for a moment, Jake studied the house and tried to sort out his plan. Through a front window, he could see lights on inside. Someone was home. Was it Judd? Jake got out of his truck and as calmly as possible walked up the sidewalk toward the front of the house. He could feel his heart pounding in his chest with each step. There wasn't much activity on the street. It was late. No kids out playing. No one walking dogs. Someone looked to be working inside an open garage a few houses down the way. Jake slipped past the truck in the driveway and then cautiously poked his head around to try to peer through the front window. A small study. Nobody was in it. But Jake could hear noise from deeper in the house. Sounded like a loud TV.

Jake had no plans to use the front door, of course, so he slipped around to the side yard and made his way up to a wooden gate to the back. He wondered if Judd would have a dog. He didn't enjoy the thought of coming face-to-face with a rottweiler or the like right now. But he would certainly chance it. He flipped the latch on the gate, cracked it open, and then slid into the dark backyard. Then he crept along the side of the house and peeked around a corner. It was a small, barren backyard. There were a couple of nets hung up in trees with footballs lying around in the grass. Thankfully, no signs of any dogs anywhere.

Jake scooted along the back of the house, under a window, until he was a few feet away from a tiny back patio with two plastic lawn chairs, a rusty grill, and a plastic garbage can overflowing with crushed beer cans. Jake now had a clear view into the family room through an oversize window. A large TV showed a football game. And there was Judd McGee, slouched in a leather recliner in front of it, wearing only a pair of blue jeans with no shirt. A TV tray next to the recliner was littered with beer cans. Jake didn't see anyone else in the house but then noticed a light was on in a window on the other side of the patio. Was Judd's son, Quinn, home? Jake hadn't noticed the boy's truck out front. He watched as Judd suddenly got up out of the recliner and made his way down a hallway toward the location of the light.

Crouching down, Jake carefully scooted across the yard and over to where he could see the light on inside. It was likely a bedroom, but the window was covered with cheap blinds. Still, he had a small sliver of a peek inside. And what he saw sent a jolt right through him: *Piper!* He'd found her. He couldn't believe it. She was right there in front of him, sitting on a bed, back to the window, arms tucked around her legs in a tight ball. Judd said something to her with a scowl, turned off the light, and then shut the bedroom door.

With his adrenaline kicking into high gear, Jake raced over to the back patio door. This time, he wasn't sneaking around. The patio door wasn't locked. Not that it mattered—Jake would have knocked the damn thing down to get inside right now. Judd was in the process of sitting in his recliner again. Opening the door, Jake rushed into the house ready to do whatever necessary to rescue Piper from this nightmare—and from this monster of a man.

From his recliner, Judd McGee turned at the unexpected intrusion, muttered, "What the hell . . ."

But before Judd could even make a move, Jake lunged at him. They both toppled over the recliner onto the tattered carpet. Filled with rage, Jake jumped on top of Judd. His right fist hit the man solid on the jaw, knocking his head sideways. Jake followed that up with a left and then another right. Judd was not putting up much of a fight. He just tried to hold his hands up in front of his face to keep from being punched. The man smelled like he was drenched in alcohol.

"How could you do this!" Jake yelled.

"Do . . . what?"

No longer punching, Jake put his right hand around Judd's neck and squeezed. "Who else is here?"

For the first time, Judd seemed to recognize him. "Coach Slater . . . what the . . . ?"

"Who else is here?" Jake repeated, squeezing harder.

Judd tried to answer through the choking. "What . . . uh, no one . . . I mean, only my stepdaughter."

Jake heard a sudden scream come from behind him. He spun around, found a brown-haired girl around the same age and stature as Piper standing in the hallway with a look of horror on her face. And that's when Jake realized he'd made a huge mistake. It was not Piper he'd seen through the crack in the blinds. It was a different girl. And she looked terrified at seeing a strange man choking her stepfather. Jake quickly pulled his hand away from Judd's throat. How could he have made that mistake? Did he only see what he wanted to see through the blinds? Had his fear and panic tricked his own mind and led him to make a foolish assumption?

Jake stared back down at Judd. "Piper isn't here?"

Judd was massaging his throat. "Who . . . ?"

"My daughter!"

"Why the hell would your daughter be here? What's wrong with you?"

The man's speech was severely slurred. He was clearly drunk. Jake felt his entire theory about Judd swiftly unraveling on him. Given the man's current state, and the fact that he had his stepdaughter home with him, Jake thought it was highly unlikely Judd could've been the same guy who'd snatched Piper earlier. And that's when a new wave of fear overtook him. If not Judd, then who? Where was his daughter?

"I'm sorry," Jake said, standing up. He then turned to the girl. "I'm so sorry. Don't be afraid. This was a terrible mistake. Everything is going to be OK."

Without explaining himself further, Jake hurried toward the front door of the house. Once outside on the front sidewalk, he felt all his emotions boil to the surface. Feeling sick again, he hunched over and vomited what little he still had left in his stomach.

FIFTEEN

Jake parked his truck in an empty lot in front of a closed hardware store. His heart was still racing from the mix-up at Judd's house a few minutes ago. He hoped his actions wouldn't traumatize that little girl for life. Jake had acted rashly and now questioned his own judgment. He'd beaten up an innocent man. Jake wondered if Judd had called the police on him right after he'd left. Just in case, Jake decided he should change things up yet again. Opening the black theater kit, he found a second small bottle of adhesive removal. The instructions said to gently dab it behind the fake hair with a brush and gradually peel away the fake facial hair. He did just that until the mustache was gone. To replace it, he chose a salt-and-pepper gray goatee set. Just like before, he used the spirit gum to apply the new facial hair and then studied himself in the rearview mirror. The goatee was slightly off-center, but serviceable. He didn't need to make it perfect.

Sitting there in the truck, Jake tried to sort out his next move. If not Judd, then who was behind all this—and why? What truth could Piper possibly know? Jake had angered a lot of people in the community last year with the way the football season had unfolded. There were so many parents and fans who had voiced their severe displeasure with him. But he couldn't imagine anyone other than Judd responding in a way that nearly put his whole family in the grave. It didn't make any sense to him. Could it have been something else? Could Sarah have somehow been the catalyst behind all this? Or Caitlin? Or Piper? If Jake could find the right tow-truck company, maybe he could somehow track down the driver from tonight. But that would be a challenge. His sole focus earlier had been on catching up to the black truck, not paying enough attention to company brandings or other identifiable markings. He regretted that now. But he remembered one clear identifier for sure. The tow truck had a *Geaux Tigers* purple-and-gold LSU sticker on the back bumper. It wasn't much to go on, but it was all he had at the moment.

Using his burner phone, Jake began searching the internet for local tow-truck companies to see if he could find a possible match. The first search result felt like a knee to the groin. There were more than one hundred different towing companies listed in and around Austin. He shook his head. One by one, Jake searched through websites looking for images that showed off their trucks. Many of the companies did not have websites, which made his hunt feel even more futile. After thirty minutes of connecting dots, Jake came up with a list of twenty-one different possibilities. Each of the towing companies on his list used some version of black tow trucks. They were all over the city. It might take him all night to track them all down. But it was the only way forward he could think to take right now, and he certainly wasn't going to be sleeping anyway.

Pulling out of the parking lot, Jake set off to visit each location on the list. While many of the towing companies advertised being open twenty-four hours, Jake figured this was after-hours, by telephone only, as all he found with each successive stop were locked, dark buildings. But thankfully, there were tow trucks parked in and around most of these sites that allowed him to take some inventory. However, after more than three hours of driving around town, Jake still had not found a match for the LSU bumper sticker. He was starting to lose any hope of this working. But stop number seventeen changed the story: A & Z Wrecker and Recovery.

The building was basically a run-down mobile home sitting on about an acre of land in industrial East Austin surrounded by other business strips and complexes. The lights were off in the building, and no one was around. Jake stood at a chain-link security fence behind the building and from a distance stared at four different black tow trucks parked side by side. It sure as hell looked like one of them had a *Geaux Tigers* bumper sticker.

Reaching up, Jake began climbing the chain-link security fence, pulled his legs over, and then found himself back on the pavement on the other side. He hustled over to the short row of tow trucks. His heart rate jumped. It was indeed the same bumper stick he'd spotted earlier. The truck looked like the exact same model, too. He'd found the vehicle—he felt certain of it. Both doors were locked on the truck. Jake peered into the windows to see if he could spot anything inside that might tell him who the driver was tonight. He didn't see anything lying around that might be useful. No company name tags or lanyards. No magazines with subscription labels. The cabin of the tow truck was very clean. He thought about breaking the window and searching the glove box but decided against it. Someone nearby might hear him and call the police.

Jake stood there a moment, wondering what to do next. How would he go about identifying the driver? The company website didn't list anyone specifically. Looking at his phone, he decided to dial the phone number for the tow-truck company. Maybe he could talk his way into information. It was nearly two in the morning. Could he expect to get an answer at this hour? The phone rang four times and went to an automated company voice mail, asking callers to leave a message about their situation; someone would call back shortly. He left a quick message: "Yeah, my name is Jeff. I need a tow ASAP. Call me back, please." He went on to leave his new phone number. He thought about saying someone was on-site breaking into their building, like he was an eyewitness or something, and telling them they should get down here right away. But again, Jake was concerned about potential police involvement.

Climbing back over the security fence, Jake returned to the front side of the building. He wondered if he should find some way to break in and have a look around. The door had a sticker on it claiming the building was guarded by an alarm system and a security company. Was that true? By the looks of things, he highly doubted it. But it wasn't a risk he wanted to take right now. He called the phone number for the towing company a second time and left an even more urgent message, begging them to call back. He then paced in a circle in front of the building for about twenty minutes before he lost all hope of a return phone call tonight. Still, he wasn't leaving this place until someone called him back or showed up in the morning. He had no other leads to pursue. The man who drove that tow truck held Jake's whole life in his hands.

SIXTEEN

The Gulfstream G450 touched down on a private strip at Austin–Bergstrom International Airport at 4:22 a.m. The pilot then taxied into an empty hangar where a white Range Rover and a black Ford Taurus sat parked next to each other. There was only one passenger on the flight. He'd been picked up at a private airstrip in New Jersey a few hours ago. His name was Logan Gervais. Born in Quebec, he was once a promising Canadian federal agent specializing in cyberterrorism. Gervais was as skilled with the computer as he was with his gun. But he'd left his government position ten years ago to become an independent contractor in New York City. He was best known around Manhattan as the Ghost because of his uncanny ability to appear and disappear in the most impossible places to get a job done. Gervais hadn't come up with the name himself—a client who wanted a business competitor eliminated gave it to him—but he certainly loved it.

As the jet came to a stop, Gervais remained sitting in his plush leather seat, sipping a cup of coffee while staring out the window at the two parked vehicles. At five nine and 160 pounds with close-cropped brown hair, Gervais looked more like an accountant than a hit man—which, of course, played well for him in his work. It was unusual for him to take a job on such short notice, much less get on a plane at such an obscenely early hour. But this client had agreed to pay more than double his normal retaining fee, so he said yes. Plus, he liked Austin. He'd been there a couple of times over the years for music festivals. There was also a Formula One race scheduled for the coming week. Gervais thought he might hang around town after he finished and check it out.

The pilot came out of the cockpit, opened the cabin door, lowered the stairs, and left the plane. A minute later, a sixtysomething man in a black suit got out of the Range Rover, walked over to the plane, and boarded. The pilot remained outside. Gervais recognized the man in the suit as the same lawyer who'd worked the proper back channels to contact him. This man was not the client, but he worked for the client—this was usually how these things were done. He rarely met face-to-face with the powerful and wealthy individuals who wanted someone dead. Sometimes Gervais wasn't even sure who was paying the bill—which didn't really matter to him as long as the money was transferred into his account.

"Mr. Gervais, my name is Nelson Wyatt. I spoke with you on the phone earlier. Thank you for coming here so quickly."

"Do you have everything I requested?"

Wyatt nodded. "I had a car delivered. It's waiting outside for you. I just sent the digital file to the encrypted link you forwarded to me earlier. Everything you wanted should be in there. If not, please do let me know."

"Very good. As I mentioned before, the remainder of the money must be wired to my account within twenty-four hours of completion."

"Yes, if you complete it within the time frame we discussed, it will be there."

Gervais gave him a half smile. "I can assure you, I will complete it."

Wyatt looked nervous. Gervais liked that.

"Is there anything else you need at this time?" Wyatt asked.

"No, you can go now."

Wyatt nodded and backed out of the plane like he was afraid Gervais might shoot him in the back. Gervais found it humorous how people would often act around him—like he was some kind of psycho who ran around and shot everyone in sight. The truth couldn't be more different. Gervais was just a businessman with a unique skill set and an unusual service to offer. Reaching down beside him, he grabbed his leather backpack and pulled it into his lap. Unzipping it, he lifted his laptop out and then opened it up on a small tabletop in front of him. A few clicks later, he was inside an encrypted website he used for jobs like this one.

The digital file the lawyer had mentioned was in place. Gervais opened it and began to examine the information. There were several photos of his target. He was a handsome everyman type of guy a few years older than himself. There was also a long list of known friends, associates, and other contacts his client thought were important. Gervais would immediately put his covert online skills to work on each of the individuals on the list. If the target reached out to one of them through any of the usual means, Gervais would know and be able to quickly respond. This was how he did his job better than anyone else.

Sitting back, Gervais again studied a photo of the man. He wondered what this poor guy could have possibly done to deserve a meeting with the Ghost. He wasn't an important politician, government leader, or even a high-profile businessman, like most of his usual targets. What kind of client paid half a million dollars to eliminate a high school football coach?

SEVENTEEN

Dani rolled over in her bed and stared bleary-eyed at the alarm clock going off on her nightstand. Six thirty? She'd been in bed for only about three hours. Why the hell had she set an alarm clock? She reached over and slapped the top of the clock to shut it off, which didn't work. That's when she realized it was actually her cell phone continuing to blast away beside it. Someone was incessantly calling her. Pulling herself up, she sighed heavily and then turned on her nightstand lamp. This made Bailey perk up beside her. Great. Now she would have to get up and take the dog out. Dani grabbed her cell phone and squinted at the screen. Special Agent Eric Mitchell.

"Do you ever sleep, Mitchell?" Dani answered.

"As little as possible."

"This had better be good."

"You ever heard of a hit man up in New York City they call the Ghost?"

Dani rubbed her face with her free hand. "Uh . . . the Ghost? No . . . wait . . . Is that the guy they suspect took out the deputy mayor there three years ago for the Moraldo family—or something like that?"

"Yep. Same guy. Real name is Logan Gervais."

"Why are we talking about a ghost at six thirty in the morning?"

"I just got off the phone with New York. They've been hunting this guy *forever*. He works in the shadows and has been nearly impossible to track. But they finally found a crack about twelve hours ago. They said Gervais got on a private plane out of Jersey to Austin during the middle of the night."

"Do they want us to grab him?"

"No, they don't want us to touch him. They want the Moraldo family. So they are handling this with incredibly delicate gloves right now to see if they can somehow hack his online network and make a direct connection. But they felt obligated to inform us of his arrival."

"Why?"

"He's here for a job, Dani. New York intercepted an encrypted file. You're never going to guess the proposed target."

"I'm too tired to guess. Just tell me already."

"Jake Slater."

This made Dani pop straight up out of bed. "What?"

"Yeah, exactly. I thought this was worth waking you up."

"You thought right. So . . . who hired him?"

"We don't know yet. But I just sent you a link to a security video from a private hangar over at Austin–Bergstrom from about two hours ago."

"All right, give me a second." She searched her phone and found the text from Mitchell. The link took her to a secured video source. As Mitchell mentioned, the video looked to be from a security camera in the corner of an oversize airport hangar. "I'm watching now."

"OK, good. I edited the video to take out blocks of stagnant time. You can keep track from the time stamp in the corner."

Dani noticed that two vehicles were parked in view inside the hangar: a white Range Rover and a black Ford Taurus. Then a private jet eased into the hangar and parked next to the vehicles. A pilot lowered the stairs and got off the plane. Then a man in a dark suit climbed out of the Range Rover and boarded the jet. Within minutes, he returned to his vehicle and drove off. Ten minutes later, a man she guessed was Logan Gervais exited the plane. He settled into the black Taurus and also drove away. Then the pilot backed the jet out of the hangar and moved out of camera view.

"Who's the guy in the suit, Mitchell?"

"No idea. Still unidentified. I'm sending you enhanced close-up still shots right now."

Dani again checked her phone and opened the images. The guy was a gray-haired individual probably in his early sixties. "Were you able to get the plates?"

"Unfortunately not. I'm trying to see if there are other cameras around there that might've captured the vehicles from better angles."

"The plane still at the airport?"

"No, it immediately took off. I think headed to the Bahamas."

"Damn. But I do know a guy down there. Someone I used to work with in DC. Retired now. Maybe I can get him to do me a favor and find the pilot after he lands. Whose plane is it?"

"Belongs to one of those shared programs for high rollers. Called Wheels in the Air. So it's used by a lot of different companies and clients."

"Do we know which one chartered the flight and picked up this guy in New Jersey?"

"Not yet. Can't get anyone on the phone there."

"OK, keep me posted."

"What do you think is going on here, Dani?"

"No clue. You got anything else for me?"

"Yeah, one more thing. I tracked down the guy from the bar last night that multiple eyewitnesses said Jake Slater was talking to when we arrived. Woke him up a few minutes ago and spoke with him. His name is Drew Beamer. He's the head football coach at the same high school where Slater used to work. I guess they're old friends or something. Anyway, he claims Slater texted him late last night and asked to meet.

They were only together for a couple of minutes. The coach said Slater was trying to find a guy named Judd McGee, who I guess is the father of one of the players he used to coach. Beamer claims he doesn't know why Slater was trying to find him. Beamer gave him an address for McGee and some cash, and that was it, he says. Other than he believes Slater is innocent."

"You get the address for McGee?"

"Yeah. He lives down in East Austin."

"OK, text it over. I'll meet you there in about thirty minutes or so."

"Copy that. I'll have coffee waiting."

"Thanks. I'll need it."

Dani hung up, stood there in shock. How could Jake possibly be the target of an infamous hit man who had been flown in overnight from New York? Who would want him dead?

What was really going on here?

EIGHTEEN

Jake half dozed while sitting in his truck but never really slept—even though he was physically and emotionally exhausted. There was no way for him to shut down the pulsing fear he was carrying around inside him. Every time he closed his eyes, he heard Piper screaming: *Daddy!* He doubted he would ever be able to sleep again if he didn't get his daughter back. After all, he'd promised to be there for her always. If he broke that promise, Jake didn't think he'd survive. Losing Sarah had devastated him. But losing Piper would destroy him.

As the sun started to rise on the day, Jake watched a beat-up gray Ford F-150 pull directly in front of the company's portable building. An overweight man probably in his midtwenties wearing a camouflage hunting jacket, blue jeans, and cowboy boots got out of the truck. There was no way this was the same guy who got into the tow truck with Piper last night. That man was much thinner. Jake had wondered if there'd be a slim chance he'd come face-to-face with his daughter's captor this morning.

As the heavy guy made his way up to the front of the building, Jake got out of his truck, hurried up a sidewalk, and then entered the small parking lot behind him. Jake had changed back to the brown knit ski cap and fake square-rimmed glasses—along with his new gray goatee.

Even with the disguise, he wondered if the guy in the camouflage jacket might still recognize him from all the TV news coverage last night. How many people paid close attention to that kind of thing? He never did. But it still made his heart beat a little faster just at the possibility. Jake had to be prepared for anything—even hauling ass out of there. The guy was at the door of the building, fiddling with keys, but turned as Jake approached him.

"You work here?" Jake said, with a certain authority in his voice. He'd rehearsed this repeatedly throughout the night.

The guy nodded. "Yep. What's up?"

Jake pulled a thin black wallet from his pocket and flipped it open like he'd practiced, flashing a fake police detective badge from the high school drama department's props. "Detective Connors, APD. I need to ask you a few questions."

He quickly shut the wallet, stuffed it back in his pocket. Jake had a more aggressive step ready if the man wanted to examine the badge more closely or began to ask more probing questions. But thankfully, it didn't look like he was going to have to go to plan B. The guy seemed to buy it.

"What kind of questions?" the guy asked.

"We're investigating an incident from last night involving one of your drivers. I need to get a name and contact info from you."

"An incident? What happened?"

"Can't really tell you that, or it might jeopardize our investigation."

"Uh, OK."

"First, I need your name."

"Gary Stromberg."

"How long you worked here, Gary?"

"'Bout four years or so."

"And what's your job?"

"I help run scheduling for Mr. McDonnell, the owner. Manage maintenance for our trucks and stuff like that."

"So you know all the drivers?"

"I do." His forehead suddenly bunched. "Was it Bubba? That dude is always causing us problems. I keep telling Mr. McDonnell to fire him."

"Was Bubba driving last night?"

"I think so. Let me double-check."

After unlocking the door to the building, Gary walked inside, and Jake followed him. As he suspected, there was no real alarm system since Gary didn't punch numbers on any keypads. The small building was just an open room with several desk stations and a restroom at one end. After flipping on the lights, Gary ambled over to one of the desks and lowered his substantial girth into an office chair behind a computer on a messy desk. He punched on a keyboard and a few seconds later had some answers for Jake.

"Yeah, Bubba was working last night," Gary confirmed.

"Was he driving the truck with the LSU bumper sticker?"

Gary rolled his eyes. "Archie put that damn sticker on there. Mr. McDonnell keeps telling him to take it the hell off. My boss loves Alabama and hates LSU." He poked at his keyboard some more. "No, that truck was not actually on the schedule last night. You sure you got the right vehicle?"

"I'm sure. It was clearly identified."

"Well, I don't know what to tell you. If it was out, it was unauthorized."

"Who else has access to the property and the trucks?"

"All of our drivers do. There's a combo lock on the gate. Truck keys are kept in a lockbox behind the building."

"So any one of them could've come here and taken out one of your trucks even if they were not scheduled to drive?"

"I suppose. But they'd get fired for doing something like that."

"How many drivers do you have?"

"Eight part-time guys that rotate on the schedule."

"Then I'm going to need the names and contact information for each of them."

Gary wrinkled his brow. "Well, I, uh, probably need to check in with Mr. McDonnell first. I mean, I don't want to get into any trouble here."

"I wouldn't do that. Because that will only turn this into a much bigger ordeal. It'll be a real hassle for both of us. Honestly, I'll probably have to lock down this whole facility for a while as part of the investigation."

"Damn. Really?"

"Yeah. I just need a list, Gary. Then you probably won't see me again."

"Yeah, all right." Gary typed on his keypad again and printed something off the cheap printer behind his desk. He then handed it over to Jake.

Jake quickly scanned it and wondered which of these guys might have shot Caitlin and taken his daughter. Not a single name on the list meant anything to him. "Hey, save me some time here. The driver in question was a slender guy. About my height."

"Then you can scratch off Bubba, Marcus, and Ned. Those guys are even fatter than me, if you can believe that. You can probably also scratch off Lewis. He's a short dude. Probably only five foot five."

"That's helpful." Jake headed for the door but then thought of something else and turned back. "Hey, one more quick question for you, Gary. Was one of your tow trucks involved in a major crash a little over a year ago?"

Gary leaned back in his office chair. "A year ago?"

"Yeah. November 10, to be exact."

"Is this related to last night?"

"Maybe. I don't know yet. But am I right?"

"Actually, yeah. I mean, I can't remember the exact date, but it was around the time you mentioned. Did about three thousand dollars in damage to the front."

"Who was the driver involved?"

"Eddie Cowens. Said a deer made him swerve off the road."

Jake glanced at the paper in his hands. Eddie's name was on the list. He'd actually found the guy. Eddie's address was the same zip code as the tow company, which meant his place was nearby. The thought of potentially having Piper safely back in his arms within minutes shot a bolt of adrenaline straight through him.

"Thanks," he said, darting for the door.

NINETEEN

Logan Gervais did a quick pass through the middle-class neighborhood in his black Ford Taurus. He wanted to get his bearings and process his options of escape should he have to quickly get away from the one-story white brick house he'd set eyes on a few minutes ago. He wanted to get in and out, especially because daylight was now putting him out in the open. Based on the text message he'd just monitored, Gervais knew he could have unwanted company here soon. The message had originated from someone on his list and went directly to his target's cell phone, which was no longer in service.

Drew Beamer: Hey, bud, the FBI was just here asking about you. I told them you were looking for Judd McGee last night, and I gave you his address. I'm sorry. I didn't know what to do. This is crazy. Just wanted to give you a heads-up. Be careful out there, man.

After getting the lay of the land, Gervais returned near the house and parked on the curb two blocks away. He'd changed into a gray jogging outfit, running shoes, and a black knit cap. He looked like an early-morning runner. Before getting out of the car, he tugged on a pair of thin black gloves. It was cold out, and the gloves were appropriate for the occasion—but they, of course, had the secondary benefit of leaving no prints.

He reached down to a small black metal box sitting in the passenger seat and opened it. Inside, he grabbed his gun and the silencer barrel and quickly attached the two together. Then he stuffed it into a hidden waist holster under his jogging pants for safekeeping. One more quick glance up and down the street. It was apparently trash day in the neighborhood, which was irritating—it meant more activity on the street. He spotted several neighbors hauling green trash containers from their garages down to the curb. Most folks were still in their sleepwear.

Getting out of the Ford Taurus, Gervais stretched his back for a moment, then started a slow jog up the street. He covered the two blocks and then slowed as he approached the one-story white brick house with the oversize pickup truck parked out front. He hadn't spotted any activity in or around the house this morning during his drive back and forth earlier. He circled the truck, took one last peek behind him to make sure no neighbors were watching, and then went straight for the front door. He felt no need to sneak in the back. Reaching down to the door handle, he found it appropriately locked. Which was not a problem. He quickly pulled a small tool out of his right pocket, knelt, inserted the tool into the key slot, and a second later, he had the dead bolt shifted to open. He'd done this hundreds of times with much more complex locking systems.

Pulling his gun out of his waist holster and holding it in his right hand, Gervais reached down with his left and cracked open the front door. He was prepared to move quickly if the house had an alarm system and started beeping with its warning. He'd have no trouble disarming a simple alarm. But based on the condition of the house, he doubted that would be the case. He was right. There were no sounds as he pushed open the front door. He wondered if there would be a barking dog. He had a bullet ready to silence any mutts that threatened his job. He took no pleasure in shooting dogs—he was a dog lover himself and had two beautiful pit bulls back in New York—but he had to do what he had to do to complete the assignment.

He slipped inside, swiftly shut the door behind him. Standing there, he listened for sounds of movement in the house. Nothing. Nobody was up and moving around. No dogs rushing toward the front door. That should make this much easier. He'd rather deal with only one specific person while he was here this morning. He moved past a study on his left and down a short hallway toward a living room and kitchen. Gervais made note of all the empty and crushed beer cans sitting around a beat-up recliner in the living room. There was an opened pizza box on a coffee table. A glance in the kitchen. Disgusting. A stack of dirty dishes piled high in the sink. Several fast-food bags sitting on the counters. More beer cans. Gervais was getting a quick education on what he might be dealing with in a few minutes. The guy was a sloppy drunk and would likely be hungover. That could be good or bad, depending on how coherent he was this morning. Gervais checked his watch. He needed to get moving.

Another short hallway led to the bedrooms. The first door was closed. Gervais cracked it open, peeked inside. He spotted a girl in maybe her early teens sleeping soundly in the bed. He closed the door, kept moving. The next bedroom had a messy bed, but no one was lying in it. The walls were covered with sports posters and girls in bikinis. Probably belonged to a teenage boy who wasn't home. As he approached the end of the hallway and the final bedroom, Gervais could hear heavy snoring. Sounded like a man. But was anyone with him? Wife? Girlfriend? He'd rather not have to deal with an extra set of eyes and ears this morning, but again, he was prepared to do whatever was necessary to get the information he needed.

The door to the master bedroom was open. Gervais crept inside, surveyed the king-size bed, and smiled. Only one person was in the bed. A skinny fortysomething guy with a goatee. The covers were kicked way down on the bed. The guy was bare-chested and still wearing blue jeans. He'd probably passed out that way. Gervais moved to the side of the bed, reached down with his gun, and placed the silencer barrel on the man's forehead. Then he tapped hard three times. The guy kind of grunted, cursed, his eyes fluttering open. When he realized there was a man standing over him with a gun pointed at his face, his eyes shot wide open with sudden panic.

"Good morning," Gervais said, flashing a sinister grin.

"What the . . . ?"

"Stay calm," Gervais instructed. "We don't want to wake up the girl down the hallway, do we?"

The man stiffened, fear spreading down the length of his body. Gervais was used to seeing this very reaction. He'd woken many targets in this same manner.

"You are Mr. McGee?" Gervais asked.

"Who are you?"

Gervais moved the gun slightly and pulled the trigger. The muffled bullet took off the man's left earlobe, making him jerk back and grab his now-bloody ear with a yelp.

"I ask the questions, not you," Gervais said. "One more time. You are Mr. McGee?"

The man quickly nodded, clutching his left ear with his left hand. Blood was covering his fingers.

"Do you know someone named Jake Slater?"

Another quick nod.

"When was the last time you saw him?"

"Uh, last night. He came to my house."

"Good. What time?"

"I, uh, I don't remember."

Gervais shifted the gun again, pulled the trigger, and took off the man's right earlobe. The guy groaned, jerked again, and now had both hands pressed to the sides of his head.

"I need you to think more clearly, Mr. McGee," Gervais said. "This is important to me. Do you understand?"

More nodding. "It was, uh, before midnight."

"Are you sure?"

"Yes, I was, uh, watching the UCLA football game. West Coast. And it was only halftime."

"What did Mr. Slater want?"

The man swallowed, grimaced. Blood from his ears was oozing through his fingers and running down his neck. "He was acting crazy. He thought I had his daughter or something."

"Do you?"

He shook his head. "No. I, uh . . . I didn't know what he was talking about."

"What else did he say?"

"I mean, nothing, really."

Gervais cocked his head, as if a warning.

This sent panic through the man's eyes. "I swear! He just started apologizing. My stepdaughter came in, and he apologized to her, too. Said he made a big mistake. And then he left, and that was it. I swear to God. That's all of it."

Gervais studied the man. He was telling the truth. The piss stain now forming in the front of the man's blue jeans told him that.

"OK, you have a good day," Gervais said.

He turned and began walking back toward the hallway. But then he heard sudden movement from behind him. Spinning back around, Gervais found the guy scrambling to reach under his bed. Then the man put his hand on a gun and began lifting it out into the open. Gervais rolled his eyes, aimed his own gun, and fired off two shots. They both hit the man directly in the center of the forehead, and he plopped back onto the mattress.

"Idiot." Gervais sighed, and left.

TWENTY

Jake parked on the side of a dirt road surrounded by open fields in deep East Austin and stared up ahead of him at a run-down RV that sat alone on a couple of acres of unkempt land. It was a setup similar to other trailers and mobile homes he'd passed along this same route for more than a mile. He studied the digital dot on the map on his burner phone. According to the map, this was Eddie Cowens's place—whom Jake now believed to be the driver of the tow truck who killed Sarah in the hit-and-run crash last year and took Piper from Caitlin's house.

Who the hell was this guy? Jake had spent several minutes searching the internet for info on the man. There was barely anything out there on his name. The guy didn't participate in social media, as far as Jake could tell, and he wasn't part of any club, organization, or business that had once published details on the web. Eddie Cowens was a no one—so how had the man become the center of a tornado that had destroyed Jake's whole world?

Jake eased his vehicle forward. As he did, he noticed a small white barn with a metal roof appear behind the RV. It was more like a shack, but still—could Piper be inside? His heart started pumping faster. Was this where they were holding her hostage? There were no vehicles currently on the property. If someone was here, they were without a car.

After parking his truck in the grass beside the dirt road, Jake got out and surveyed the entire landscape, just so he had his bearings. He had no idea what was about to happen when he approached the trailer and the barn. He wanted to be ready for anything. Up ahead of him about a quarter mile down the dirt road, he noticed a guy on a huge tractor working in a field. But that was the only person he'd seen in the general vicinity.

Walking toward the RV, Jake felt exposed out in the open and hoped the potential of being spotted wouldn't jeopardize whatever chances he had of rescuing Piper. If someone was inside the trailer or barn and spotted him, would they move quickly to do something to his daughter? But he had no choice. There was no other way to sneak up to the property. He walked even faster.

Jake wished he had some kind of weapon on him. There was nothing in his backpack that would help him with any physical encounter. He just had his fists. Cutting through the grass toward the trailer, Jake came upon a rusted-out old riding lawn mower stuck in dirt with weeds as tall as the mower all around it. There was other trash and junk littered throughout the front yard. Searching the ground, Jake spotted a rusted metal bar of some kind and picked it up. It was at least something with which to take a swing, if necessary.

Slowing down as he got within ten feet of the RV, Jake began to listen more closely. He didn't hear any sounds coming from inside. No TV, no radio, no talking. But it was only seven thirty in the morning. Someone could still be asleep. The windows on the RV were too high to peer through. Still, he studied each window to see if he spotted a light on inside. Every one of them looked dark. Jake slowly circled the trailer, hand gripped on the metal bar. The backyard was more junked up than the front yard. There was a burned-up metal barrel with ashes pouring out surrounded by two metal folding chairs and a huge collection of beer cans and bottles. There was an old truck with no tires, a missing hood, and other parts sitting in the dirt over to his left. Sidling up close to the RV, Jake again listened closely. He still didn't hear anything from inside the trailer. So he decided to move toward the small white barn. With each step, his adrenaline pumped a little quicker. *God, please let Piper be inside, safe and sound.*

There was an opening in the barn. As he quickly approached, Jake spotted another vehicle inside the small building sitting in the dirt with no tires. Looked like an old Buick. Stepping up to the opening, Jake took a cautious peek around the corner. His shoulders sagged. It was basically empty. Only two metal shelves filled with junk sat along one wall and a stack of hay squares in the corner. No Piper. He searched the entire barn to see if he could spot any signs that his daughter might have once been held inside. But nothing stood out to him.

Leaving the barn, Jake hustled back over to the RV. He stepped up onto a small attached patio to move toward the front door. Again, he paused to listen. Still no sounds coming from inside. He knocked on the door, gripped his metal bar fiercely in his right hand, ready to strike. But no one came to the door. He pounded again, even louder. Still no response. Reaching down, Jake tried to turn the doorknob, but it was locked. He had no plans to let that stop him from getting a look around inside. Using the metal bar, he shoved it into the crack between the door and the doorjamb. Then he started jimmying it as hard as he could. The door held for a moment, but it was cheap material. The more Jake worked the metal bar with his full strength, the looser the door got. Until it finally tore the lock apart from the doorjamb. He was inside the filthy trailer a moment later. It smelled something terrible. Like stale food, dirty socks, and marijuana.

Jake quickly scanned the area. A tiny kitchenette and bathroom to his left. A sitting area and a small bedroom to his right. It looked like the place had never been cleaned. Clothes were strewn all over the place. The kitchen counters were covered with dirty plates and fast-food wrappings. Jake did a quick search around to see if he'd find anything helpful. There was a framed photo of a man and woman on the kitchen counter standing somewhere together. Jake picked it up and examined it. Looked like they were at a rodeo or something. They were both probably in their mid- to late twenties. The guy had a goatee and a cowboy hat. His arm was wrapped around the girl. Staring at him, Jake thought by body type it could definitely be the same guy he'd seen at the hit-and-run crash and at his niece's house last night. He put the photo down and kept searching.

A table in the middle held three overflowing ashtrays, a stack of car magazines, and a huge pile of mail. Jake started picking through the mail and confirmed this was indeed Eddie Cowens's trailer. He quickly riffled through the various envelopes, some of which had never been opened. Most were bills. Utilities, credit cards, gas cards, a few pay stubs for A & Z Wrecker and Recovery. On the floor next to the table was a cardboard box piled high with more mail. Bills, junk mail, magazines. But then he found something that stopped him cold. He pulled it out, held it in his suddenly trembling fingers. A glossy photo of Sarah, his wife. He immediately recognized it as the same photo used on her profile page on Kingston Financial's website. He flipped it over, felt a shiver push straight through him. Their home address was written on the back. So were the make, model, and license plate number of her Lexus SUV.

Jake cursed. Sarah had been the target?

He could feel his heart begin pounding.

But why? Who would've wanted to harm her?

And why had they taken Piper a year later?

Jake quickly rummaged through the rest of the box but found nothing else of interest. He wondered what to do next. Should he wait around for Eddie to come back home? Would the man show up around here at some point today? Jake could hear the sound of the tractor from up the street growing louder outside the trailer. Pushing open the door, he noticed the man on the tractor driving along the dirt road. Stepping out, Jake hustled over to flag the old man down. The tractor driver looked to be in his seventies with a long white beard and wearing blue jean coveralls. Spotting Jake, the man came to a stop in the dirt road, turned off the tractor, and peered down at him.

"You all right?" the old man asked.

"Yes, sir. Sorry to stop you like this, but I was wondering if you knew the man who lived here in the trailer."

"Eddie? Sure, I know him. He's been here about two years."

"Have you seen him around lately?"

The old man shook his head. "Not in the past couple of days. He comes and goes. Sometimes I don't see him for a while."

"Any idea where he goes when he's not here?"

The tractor driver shrugged. "No clue. He mostly keeps to himself. We chat here and there, mostly about nothing. I don't really know Eddie too well."

"But you for sure haven't seen him in a couple of days?"

"Nope. And I drive up and down this here dirt road on my tractor every single day. Eddie in trouble or something?"

"Nah, I'm just an old friend trying to find him. I sure do appreciate the help."

"You bet. Have yourself a good day."

Jake stood there as the old man drove off on the tractor. For a second, he thought about calling the phone number listed for Eddie on the contact list he'd gotten from the tow company earlier. If Eddie answered, could he possibly bargain for the release of Piper? However, Jake had only about a hundred bucks left in his pocket. Not much to bargain with, and he didn't have access to his bank accounts without the debit card in his wallet. Plus, he feared that if Eddie recognized he'd been exposed, he might do something drastic with Piper. Jake didn't want to take that chance. But if Eddie hadn't been around his trailer for a couple of days, Jake also didn't have any motivation to wait around here for him to return.

Again, he thought about the possibility that Sarah was at the center of all this. Who could've wanted her dead? Had Sarah known she was in danger? Thinking back, Jake couldn't recall anything she'd said or done leading up to the night of the crash that made him pause. Of course, at the time, he'd been completely consumed with his own world of mounting football losses, an angry fan base, and an administration wavering in their support. There was also a distance between him and Sarah, so he might not have been able to pick up on whether something was off in her world.

But Jake did know someone who would have.

Her best friend, Jill.

TWENTY-ONE

Dani took more than forty minutes to get to the address Mitchell had sent to her because her dog had no interest in expediting her morning plans by quickly going to the bathroom. When Dani finally arrived, she was troubled to find multiple police and emergency vehicles already sitting in front of the house with their lights flashing. She cursed. This couldn't be good. It was the second time in twelve hours she'd pulled up to this kind of chaotic police scene. But this was unexpected.

What the hell had happened? She swallowed a sudden knot in her throat. Could it be Jake? According to Drew Beamer, Jake was clearly on a mission to track down the resident of this house. Jake had put himself in a precarious position at the bar last night to get the address. Could something have happened to him here this morning? Another thought hit her, made her stomach turn. Could Jake have actually done something to McGee?

After parking her Mazda, Dani hustled up to the house. Mitchell was already there and waiting for her out front. He handed her a cup of coffee with a lid.

"What the hell is going on?" Dani asked him.

"We're too late."

"Too late for what?"

"He's dead."

She felt a punch to the gut. "Jake?"

Mitchell cocked his head, squinted at her. "No, Judd McGee."

Dani felt a wave of relief move through her.

Mitchell said, "Shot and killed this morning. I guess his stepdaughter found him and called the police a few minutes ago."

Dani cursed again. She had been wrong about Jake. He had actually come here and killed this man. It was hard to fathom. But why?

"How old is the stepdaughter?" she asked.

"Twelve, I think."

"Anyone else home?"

"I don't believe so. I haven't had a chance to gather much information. Just got here a few minutes before you." Mitchell again tilted his head. "What's going on, Dani? This is the second time you've called the suspect by his first name."

Dani didn't really want to lie to Mitchell. "I know the guy," she admitted.

"Seriously?"

"Or, I used to know him. Way back in the day. Haven't talked to him in forever—like fifteen years."

"Why didn't you say something?"

"It's not relevant to our investigation. Like I said, I don't have any kind of connection to the man anymore. Just knew him a long time ago."

Mitchell stared at her for another moment, clearly wanting more details, but she wasn't going to give him any.

"Let's go find out what happened," she said, moving past him.

A uniformed police officer stepped in front of her until she flashed her FBI badge in his face. He quickly stood down and let her pass. The front door was wide open. Two more officers were inside. Dani again flashed her badge.

"Who was the first on the scene?"

"Me," said one of the officers. A young guy in his late twenties.

"What's your name?"

"Officer Reed."

"Tell me what you know."

"Call came in to dispatch about fifteen minutes ago. A twelve-year-old girl met us at the front door in tears and hysterical. She's in the kitchen right now with one of our female officers. She took us to the back bedroom. We found a man dead in the bed. Shot through the head. Blood everywhere. We quickly secured the area. Waiting on crime scene to get here. That's it."

"Show me."

"The dead guy?"

"Yes."

"You sure you want to see this? It's messy."

She scowled at him. "I'm a special agent for the FBI. Not a schoolteacher."

"All right, my bad."

Dani followed him down the hallway and into the last bedroom. Stepping into the room, she found what she guessed was Judd McGee lying flat on his back in bed, blood all down his face, pooled beneath him, and soaking into the sheets.

"Must've been up close," Reed said. "Right through the forehead."

Dani stepped in even closer, studied the victim. "Two shots," she said.

"What?"

"Two shots to the head."

"How can you tell?"

"Been doing this a long time, Officer Reed."

"You can call me Nick."

She glanced at him, and he gave her a quick grin. She rolled her eyes. Nothing like a little flirting while standing in a room with a dead body. Dani leaned over the victim. She could see now that both of his earlobes were missing. That was odd. Had they been shot off? This didn't look like an act of rage or revenge to her. It looked like the work of a professional. Which made Dani immediately think about the hit man who'd just arrived in Austin only a few hours ago. Could Logan Gervais have come here? Could it have been Gervais who shot this man and not Jake?

"Dani?"

She turned. Mitchell was at the door. He waved her over.

"Damn," he said, peering around her at the victim. "Poor guy."

"Yeah, what a mess. But I don't think it was Jake Slater."

"I wouldn't be so sure."

"Why do you say that?"

"I just spoke with the stepdaughter. She says a man was here late last night. He was punching and threatening her stepdad, the victim. He stopped when she came into the room, and then he immediately took off. I showed her a photo of Slater. She ID'd him as the same guy who was here last night."

"She's sure of it?"

"Definitely. I mean, the girl is really rattled, but she seemed certain."

A new wave of police suddenly showed up at the house. Crime-scene investigators. Dani and Mitchell cleared out of the way to let them do their job. Dani was eager to find out more information on what was used to kill the victim. That would tell her a lot more about whether she believed Jake could've actually pulled the trigger. When they were dating, Jake didn't even own a gun or seem to have much interest in them. He would go to the gun range with her and watch her take target practice, but he had never had any interest in participating himself. However, that was fifteen years ago. Jake could have become an expert marksman in the time in between. But a killer? She didn't know what to think anymore—not when they knew a professional hit man was in town.

TWENTY-TWO

Jake pulled his truck up to a two-story redbrick house on a well-kept street in an upper-middle-class neighborhood called Circle C. Sarah's lifelong best friend, Jill Boetcher, lived here with her two little boys. Sarah and Jill had gone to high school together and had remained close throughout life. A divorced single mom, Jill unfortunately had been married to a real loser who eventually walked out on them. Jake had never liked the husband, but he had always enjoyed being around Jill, who worked with kids as a vice principal at a local middle school. Most of Sarah's other friends came from high society, but Jill was much more grounded and levelheaded. She'd tried her best to offer him help and comfort after Sarah's death last year. Jill even testified on his behalf during the custody battle, which had meant the world to him.

From his truck, Jake studied the front windows of the house. He thought he saw some movement going on inside. It was nearing eight in the morning. Jake knew Jill usually took her boys to church every Sunday—she had always been faithful. If they were going today, he figured they might be leaving the house soon. He did not have her phone number memorized and could find nothing listed online. And he knew he couldn't just walk up to her front door and knock. A neighbor might recognize him, even in his disguise. Several of them were out and about on the sidewalks this morning.

Plus, Jill might freak out if she pulled open the front door and saw him standing there. He had to presume she'd seen the news—his face and name had been everywhere. Considering that, Jake had no idea how receptive Jill would be to a conversation. She might immediately try to call the police. He needed to put himself in a position to test the waters with her with a quick escape route also in mind. Scooting down lower in his seat, he decided the patient route was the wisest. He would wait to see if she appeared with her boys at some point this morning and then look for an opportunity to intercept her in a nonthreatening way.

Jake again thought about the unexpected discovery of Sarah's photo inside Eddie Cowens's trailer. Did Eddie somehow know Sarah? Or had he been hired by someone else? What was the connection? And how had it led down a path of murder and kidnapping? All these questions had been on repeat in his head ever since he'd left Eddie's trailer earlier. He had to find some answers soon. The truth would likely lead him straight to Piper.

Jake waited for an hour before he finally popped up in his seat when the garage door sprang to life at Jill's house. As he'd expected, it looked like they were headed to church. Her eight- and nine-year-old boys were dressed in nice slacks, long-sleeve button-down shirts, and sweater vests. A slightly overweight blonde, Jill wore a red sweater with a long black skirt. The family of three piled into her blue minivan. Then Jill slowly pulled out of the garage, backed into the street, and drove away from the house.

Putting his truck into drive, Jake followed, looking for any opportunity to connect with her sooner rather than later. He didn't figure it would be too wise to approach her in a busy church parking lot surrounded by others. Would she take her boys out to lunch afterward? Would they be running errands? Jake's prayers were answered when Jill pulled her minivan into a gas station right outside her neighborhood.

She got out, circled her vehicle, and began working the gas pump. The pump station right behind her minivan was open. Jake eased his truck next to it. His adrenaline was flowing. It was now or never, and he just hoped Jill wouldn't lose her mind at the sight of him.

Getting out of the truck, Jake moved around toward the gas pumps. He was about fifteen feet away from Jill, who was staring at her phone while she waited for her tank to fill up. Jake took a few steps closer, and then quietly but very clearly said her name.

"Jill."

She looked up at him. At first, she didn't recognize him. But then she saw through his glasses, ski cap, and fake goatee, and her eyes went wide.

"Jake?" She gasped.

"Please don't freak out," he begged her. "I need to talk to you."

Her eyes remained wide. "Jake, the news. What is going on? The police are searching for you. Piper is missing. It was all over TV this morning."

"I know. But I swear I'm innocent. Someone else shot and killed my niece last night. And they took Piper. I'm trying to find her, Jill."

"What? Who took her?"

"I'm trying to figure that out. I need help."

"But why are the police saying you did this?"

"It's complicated. I think all of this has something to do with Sarah's death last year."

Her eyes went even bigger. "What?"

He nodded, stepped closer so he could lower his voice. "The hit-and-run last year wasn't an accident. I believe it was intentional."

"Oh my gosh. Are you serious?"

"Yes. At first, I thought I was the target. But now I believe it was Sarah. Someone was out to get her for some reason."

"Oh my . . . Sarah?"

A red Mustang pulled into the pump station across from them. A teenager got out and started working the pump. Jake stepped even closer to Jill.

"Did Sarah say anything to you in the days before she died? Something you can think of now that might be connected to all of this?"

"I . . . I don't . . . know." Jill stared off a second, thinking. "She was definitely distraught about something, Jake. She didn't tell me what it was about, but I could tell it was troubling her a lot."

"What did she say exactly?"

Jill rocked on her heels a bit. "Honestly, Jake, I think it had to do with some other guy. I hate to say it, but at the time, I wondered if she was having an affair—but I promise you I don't know anything for sure. Again, she wouldn't tell me. But the fact that she wouldn't talk about it made me suspicious. Sarah and I would talk about *everything*. We never kept secrets from each other."

Jake's head started spinning. An affair? It had never crossed his mind.

Jill added, "You guys were sort of struggling, you know."

"We were," Jake admitted. But he still couldn't process the word *affair*. Even with their struggles, he had never considered finding solace in another woman. They had built too good a life together to destroy it that way. Sarah felt the same. She'd heard and hated the rumors about her father over the years. She knew what even the rumors did to her mother. So Sarah potentially having an affair felt impossible to grasp.

"Obviously, I wasn't going to say anything to you about it after she died. What was the point? It was just speculation on my part. So I let it go. But do you think it could somehow be connected to her death?"

"I don't know. Possibly."

"Oh my gosh, Jake, this is crazy. What're you going to do?"

"Figure it out. Because I think it will lead me to Piper."

"How can I help you?"

"You've already done enough. I don't want you to get more involved."

A police car pulled up to the gas station and parked across the way. An officer got out, began walking toward the store. Jake shifted awkwardly.

"I've got to go," he said.

"Please be careful."

"I will. Thank you."

TWENTY-THREE

"What the hell, Dani? You know this guy?"

Dani stood inside her boss's office at FBI headquarters in Austin. Simon Crosby was sitting behind his desk with an exasperated look on his face. Wearing a black polo and gray slacks, he was a tall, lean man in his midforties with a close-cropped haircut that made him still look like the military man he once was. Dani and Simon had been around each other several times when she'd lived in DC, and he was there visiting for various FBI-related functions. Groups of them would always hit the bars. Simon had flirted with her from the beginning. She had sometimes flirted back. It seemed harmless at the time. They lived a thousand miles apart, so nothing serious could ever develop between them. Dani wasn't sure she ever wanted something serious again after the crushing blow of her marriage collapsing compounded her heartbreak with Jake.

But Simon had put on the full-court press as soon as she'd moved back to Austin. She was super resistant at first. After all, he was now her direct boss. And while these interoffice relationships were not completely off-limits, they were of course heavily frowned upon. But Simon was relentless, so she finally gave it a shot. It was a disaster from the beginning. To say it made her life more complicated would be an understatement. The line between boss and the guy she was dating was constantly blurred—mostly by Simon. When Dani started to feel like she was getting unfair little favors here and there, she ended it. There was no way she was going to jeopardize the respect of her peers. Simon wasn't happy about her decision and was still looking for ways to make it work between them. So she had been living in this constant tango between boss and ex-boyfriend.

"Yes," she said. "But it was a really long time ago."

Dani had felt compelled to admit her prior relationship to Jake after what had just happened to Judd McGee. She couldn't afford to play coy any longer—especially after having shared the information with Mitchell. She didn't want to put the young agent in a position of having to keep secrets. The fact that Mitchell was loyal and would do it didn't change her mind.

"How long ago?" Simon asked.

"Fifteen years. Haven't spoken to him once during that time."

"Was he just a friend or what?"

She swallowed. "Or what."

Simon frowned. "Seriously, Dani? You're telling me you used to date this guy and didn't think that was information you should have shared with me?"

"It's not relevant, Simon," she insisted. "I don't even know this guy anymore."

"Exactly. So you should have had no issue telling me about him."

"OK, my mistake. I'm telling you now."

Simon leaned back, laced his fingers together across his chest. "Were you in love with this guy?"

Dani's eyes narrowed. "Are you asking as my boss or as the guy I dated?"

"Can it be both?"

"No, it can't."

"Fine. As your boss. Are you telling me this doesn't impair your judgment?"

"Yes, that's what I'm telling you."

"One of the members on your crew said you had an open opportunity to take this guy down in the alley behind the bar last night, but you didn't. Is that true?"

"Yes, it's true. At the time, I felt it was unwarranted."

"Well, that's unfortunate. Because now another person is dead, Dani."

"I think it's questionable Jake Slater did it."

"But the stepdaughter directly ID'd him."

"She ID'd him as being in the house eight hours earlier. That's all."

"And that's all the police need to bring this guy down for it, especially when connected to the death of his niece. Have you watched the news this past hour? The police are also pinning this one on Slater. This guy is the number-one breaking news story in our city, now wanted in the deaths of two people, and we just sat there with our hands in our damn pockets."

"Let's wait until we get ballistics back."

Simon tilted his head. "You're still angling for this ghost, Gervais?"

"They were perfect kill shots, Simon. And whoever pulled the trigger took off both of the man's ears first. He was looking for information."

"OK. And that kind of work very well could've been your old boyfriend. Like you said, you don't know the guy anymore."

Dani wanted to argue with that logic, although she knew it was foolish. Truthfully, she couldn't say for sure it wasn't Jake. But she did feel like she still knew him. They had dated for two years. He'd walked her through the difficult death of her mother, who had valiantly battled cancer. Dani would have had a mental breakdown if not for the way Jake had taken care of her. He didn't leave her side for weeks. Fifteen years hadn't changed what she believed to be true of him at his core. Jake was no killer. He had always been one of the gentlest guys she'd ever been around. That's why she'd fallen in love with him. Jake was the opposite of her father, an overbearing and dominating figure. Not

physically abusive but certainly a bit of a bully who took every opportunity to put her mother in her place. Dani had always wanted to be
with someone who was nothing like her father. Jake was that guy. And
that's why it was so soul crushing when they broke up.

"You're right. I don't," Dani said. "But I still think it's peculiar."

"Well, if word leaks out to the media that we had a chance to take
this guy out and didn't, and he goes on a killing spree, it's going to be
really bad for all of us around here."

"Then do your job. And don't let word leak out."

Now she was crossing the line, and she knew it.

"Do *your* job, Dani," he retorted. "If you get another opportunity,
I'd better hear that you finished this yourself."

"You're keeping me on the investigation?"

"For now. But you're treading on very thin ice."

"Hey, don't do it as some kind of way to win me back. Do it because
it's the right decision for our department."

"That's why I'm doing it. This has become an all-out media spec-
tacle. I need it handled by the best in my department. And while
bullheaded, you're still the best agent I've got." Simon sighed. "Not
to mention this guy, Lars Kingston, could cause problems for us, if he
wanted. Kingston is clearly well connected in powerful DC circles. I've
already been forced to take multiple phone calls from him, wanting me
to keep him in the loop on our investigation. He's a real pain in the ass,
talking to me like he's my direct supervisor or something."

A quick knock on the door made Dani turn around. Mitchell was
standing there with a digital tablet in his hands.

"Sorry to interrupt," Mitchell said. "But you wanted me to come
get you as soon as I had ballistics back from the scene."

"What have you got?" Dani asked.

"It's unusual for sure. Bullets collected at the scene were Black
Talon."

Simon cursed. "Are you serious?"

"Yes, sir. Confirmed."

Dani felt a surge of relief push through her. She looked over to Simon with her palms held open in front of her, as if to say, "See? I told you so." Black Talon ammunition was known as arguably the most aggressive and lethal hollow-point round ever designed. A round that mushrooms at impact and causes incredible damage. Because of this, the ammunition had been discontinued more than twenty years ago.

Dani crossed her arms. "Something else is going on here, Simon. You know I'm right. You're telling me some football coach fired off a collection of rare bullets we can hardly find anywhere anymore?"

He glared at her. "I'm telling you to use all necessary means to bring in your ex-boyfriend, regardless of this report. Do you understand me?"

"Yes, sir."

TWENTY-FOUR

Jake drove straight to a storage facility in West Austin he'd rented to keep a lot of his old furniture, household goods, and other important personal possessions after he'd moved into his father's house four months ago. He punched in codes at a secured gate and tried to keep his face as hidden as possible from security cameras around the front entrance. His head had been spinning ever since he'd left Jill a few minutes ago.

His relationship with Sarah had started slowly fifteen years ago. Jake had still been reeling from the blow of losing Dani. Sarah had also been coming off her own bad breakup. That common ground between them had made for easy conversation. They found themselves out with friends at parties and bars but only huddled together. The attraction had always been strong. When they finally dipped their toes into a dating relationship, it didn't take long for things to begin to heat up. The fact that they came from different worlds didn't bother them at that point. They both felt it made their relationship more interesting than others. It would be a long time before cracks appeared there. Still, he loved her. He believed Sarah loved him. So how could he be sitting here pondering whether she was having an affair?

His mind had already been racing through possible candidates. There had been a few guys over the years who had always made him uncomfortable. Sarah used to date a couple of them, and—because their families were part of the Kingston inner circle—she still socialized with them quite often. The guys would sometimes make jokes around him about the one that got away. They said it with wry smiles, but he'd always sensed there was some truth in their words.

Jake parked the truck in the back corner of the storage complex. Getting out, he walked over to the two-story storage building, punched in more security codes at a back door, and entered the facility. Thankfully, there was no one else in the hallway with him. He walked down the corridor and found his specific unit. Kneeling, he entered the correct numbers on a combination lock and pulled it apart. Then he grabbed a handle on the garage-style door and lifted it all the way up. The unit was ten feet by twenty feet and stuffed full. He'd sold off most of their furniture when they were moving but kept a few items. There was his dad's old desk, an armoire he'd picked out with Sarah when they'd first married, among other assorted furniture. And then there were boxes and plastic tubs for days. Jake hadn't wanted to deal with sorting out everything a family collects over the years, so he'd just shoved it all in boxes and tubs and put it inside the unit. That was a crappy day. Mainly because Piper had been so angry with him.

"I can't believe you're making me do this," Piper said. "It's so unfair!"

They were standing in the driveway outside their West Austin house. A house where Piper had spent most of her life, and Jake had never expected to sell. A U-Haul truck was parked at the curb. Jake had been loading furniture and boxes for hours. Drew Beamer and a couple of young guys from his football team were helping him. The plan was to drive out tonight and head to Simonton, where they would live in his father's house. Piper mostly

had been sulking around and giving him death stares all day. They were get-
ting close to finishing up, and she seemed to have reached her boiling point.

"Piper, we've been over this repeatedly," he calmly said, wiping sweat
from his brow.

"I know. And it still doesn't make any sense. How could you do this
to me?"

"I'm not doing this to you. I'm doing this for us. It will be good. I
promise."

"Explain to me one more time how me moving away from my friends
is good for us."

"It's complicated. But you'll see."

She stomped her foot like a toddler. "I don't want to see! I just want
to stay!"

"I know. But you can't. I'm sorry."

Her face flushed red. "I should've chosen Grandpa and Grandma."

Her words hit him like a slap across the face. During the custody battle,
Piper had been given the opportunity to speak privately with the judge and
say whom she wanted to live with. While legally she didn't get to choose, her
personal preference would carry tremendous weight with the court's decision.
Of course, the legal proceedings never got that far after Lars backed off in
response to Jake's threats.

Piper must've been able to tell how much her words stung Jake, because her
eyes immediately filled with water. "I'm sorry, Daddy. I didn't mean it." She
rushed over and hugged him, tears streaming. "I'm so sorry. I'm just . . . scared."

"I know," Jake said. Truthfully, he was scared, too. He had no idea
where life was going to take them from here. He didn't know if he was going
to do even worse damage to Piper by forcing her to leave the only place she'd
ever known. He just knew they had to leave.

"Everything is changing so much," Piper said.

"Except us," Jake replied. "You and me. Always. Right?"

She swallowed, nodded. "Right."

Jake took a deep breath and let it out slowly. Again, he reminded himself to keep moving forward, so he began searching for a couple of specific tubs. He'd kept everything from Sarah's home office: books, notepads, journals, lamps, framed photos, and even office supplies. He'd kept all of it. But the most important items to him right now were her day planner and laptop. Jake began shifting boxes and tubs around, searching, building up a sweat while trying to make quick work of all this. It took him some time to pull everything out before he located the two tubs. He found the laptop and stepped back into the hallway to locate an electrical outlet just outside his unit. After plugging in the laptop, he set it on a stack of boxes and then powered it up. But he would need Sarah's password to get inside.

Jake went back to hunting through the two plastic tubs until he found the black day planner his wife used. Sarah was super practical. She didn't trust using only the online cloud to store her vital information. So he knew she had a page in the back of her day planner where she'd scribbled down all her important passwords and codes. Flipping through the contents of the day planner brought on a rush of emotion as he stared at his wife's handwriting and her little notes here and there. There was a family photo of them stuck in the middle of the day planner. They were skiing in Vail. Piper was eight and bundled up in her cute pink-and-purple ski jumpsuit. Tears instantly hit his eyes. The thought of going one more day without her back with him safe was nearly paralyzing. He reached up, wiped his eyes dry with his left hand, and kept searching through the day planner. He finally found the page near the back, located the password, and returned to her laptop.

He paused before typing it in. Did he really want to go here? At the moment, the prospect of an affair was just a stupid thought. Did he really want to go the distance and confirm it actually happened? Reality could be crushing. But what choice did he have? If an affair was somehow the catalyst for all this and helped him find Piper, he had to go there. He typed in her password and gained access to the laptop.

There was another family photo as her background. The three of them were celebrating at Chili's—Piper's choice—after he'd been hired as the head coach at Stephen F. Austin High School.

Jake connected to the storage facility's public Wi-Fi account and then opened up a web browser. Then he went to Google Mail, knowing Sarah used it for her personal messages. Jake had done nothing in the past year to shut down any of her email, phone, or social media accounts. The thought of closing the book on Sarah's life was just too painful. He hoped that decision would pay off for him now in finding some answers. He again searched the day-planner page for Sarah's passwords and used them to log in to her Gmail account. He could feel his heart racing with anticipation—both dread and hope. It was strange logging back in to his wife's life, as if she were still alive.

There were thousands of unread messages in her account, nearly all of which came from online stores and retail outlets where Sarah used to shop. Jake had to scroll back to a year ago to find real correspondence between his wife and other people. He finally arrived at the week of her death. Again, it was surreal to see Sarah corresponding with friends and other moms about Piper's numerous extracurricular activities. There were a few exchanges with Jake that week as they tried to manage the balance between work and home life with Piper. The exchanges seemed extra cold to him now. Like they were just partners and not a married couple. What had happened to them? How could he have let it go so far that Sarah had sought intimacy with someone else?

Jake scanned every email from the entire week but found nothing that stood out to him. There were no email exchanges with any guy that gave Jake the slightest indication that an affair might be happening. Then he thought of another direction to go. While he didn't have Sarah's cell phone, Jake did have access to all her texts through her Messages app on her laptop. He opened the app and gave it a second to load. The most recent text messages were first. There weren't many over the past year, and most of those were spam messages. Jake searched back to the week in question. There were dozens between him and Sarah; again, mostly organizing their life and running Piper around. He paused extra moments on the messages between Piper and her mom. There was a real tenderness in the text messages. Piper had lost so much last year.

He kept searching. Then Jake found a text strand that struck him hard. The contact was someone he knew well and one of the possibilities for an affair he'd thought of earlier. A successful attorney, Brent Grisham was a most-eligible-bachelor type of guy and a real charmer. Sarah and Brent had dated the year before Jake had met her. There were times when Brent was around that Jake felt he'd crossed the line in his casual flirting with his wife. Most of the texts between Sarah and Brent looked like casual banter between old friends. Some of it was about legal counsel. But it was their intimate exchange in the two days before the car crash that put Jake's heart all the way up in his throat.

Thursday. The day before the hit-and-run crash.

Brent: Hey you. You OK? You were really upset last night.

Sarah: This is hard. I don't know what to do.

Brent: I know. I'm here.

Sarah: Thanks. I'm glad.

Friday. The day of the crash.

Sarah: When can I see you again?

Brent: Tonight?

Sarah: Can't. Jake's game is tonight. Tomorrow?

Brent: Of course.

Sarah: OK. I'll text you in the morning.

Brent: Hey, be careful. This could get messy. For both of us, the way our families are so interconnected. Especially with my new job.

Sarah: I haven't told anyone. You?

Brent: No. I'm being careful.

Sarah: Same.

Jake felt his entire chest tighten up. He was suddenly having a difficult time breathing. It was one thing to ponder the possibility of an affair. It was another thing to actually see it unfolding right in front of his eyes. Why would she do this? Dumb question. He knew why. Still—it crushed him. The new job Brent had mentioned in the text exchange was a big one. Brent had been highly involved in politics for years. He and his wealthy family were well connected. His new job was being the governor's chief of staff. Jake thought about that. Could the affair somehow be connected to Sarah's death? Did Sarah know something she shouldn't? Did Piper know the truth? Had Eddie Cowens been hired by someone to keep her quiet?

Jake's mind was flooded with questions. He needed to talk to Brent. But it wasn't like he could just call up the guy and chat about this right now. And he had no idea where the guy lived. Brainstorming another strategy, Jake pulled his burner phone out of his pocket and typed in Brent's phone number. Then he punched out a message.

I know about you and Sarah Slater. We need to meet ASAP. Or I'll go straight to the media with it.

He pressed "Send," waited, hoping he would get a quick reply. He did.

Who is this? What is this about?

Jake typed out another urgent message.

Meet me at Alliance Children's Garden next to Palmer Events Center at 11. If you're not there, I swear I will ruin your career.

TWENTY-FIVE

Dani stared at a whiteboard on a wall in a small FBI conference room. She'd turned the space into a makeshift war room. The table behind her was littered with files and paperwork. The whiteboard was covered with her different scribblings as she tried to examine every intricate aspect of her investigation thus far. Jake's name was circled in the middle of the board. From there, she'd drawn lines to Caitlin Kingston's house with notes about all that had happened there last night—both the police version of events and the version Jake had told the police.

There was a line drawn to the name *Drew Beamer*, whom Jake had met downtown last night. Dani planned to speak with Drew again today to see if they had missed something about his interaction with Jake. There was a thread drawn to the dead guy, Judd McGee. Dani had been able to confirm through both the stepdaughter and two neighbors that Judd had been home all night and couldn't have been involved with what happened to Caitlin Kingston.

So why was Jake searching for him?

How had Judd McGee become a player in all this?

And why was he now dead?

Dani had drawn another line to the private plane that had landed in Austin early this morning carrying Logan Gervais—and then she'd drawn an arrow pointing from Gervais back to Judd, whom she felt certain the infamous hit man had killed. Why had Gervais been pulled into this? Did Jake know something that someone else didn't want him telling the police about?

Over on the side of the board, she'd scribbled the name *Piper Slater*, Jake's thirteen-year-old daughter. Dani had been checking in with different Kingston family members throughout the morning, and still no one had heard a peep from the girl. Where was she? The police search had turned up nothing. Did someone really take her last night? If so, who and why? How was this all interconnected? It made no sense to Dani that all this had begun to snowball last night because Jake had been upset about his niece's involvement in a custody battle over Piper that had been resolved five months ago. Something bigger was at play here, and she was determined to figure it out.

Turning around, Dani picked up a photo of Piper that she'd printed off social media. Piper was a beautiful young girl with the brightest smile, and she had Sarah's green eyes. Dani set the photo of Piper down on the conference table and picked up a photo of Caitlin Kingston. Another beautiful young woman. Such a tragedy that her life had been stolen. Dani had already spent an hour reviewing various files of paperwork Caitlin had been working on the last few weeks for the FBI. It was basic low-level administrative material. She couldn't find a single connection yet that made her believe that what happened to Caitlin last night was somehow connected to the FBI. So if this wasn't about the FBI, and it wasn't about a family custody dispute, then why had this all happened?

She again stared at the board, hoping *something* would pop out and give her new direction. But it wasn't happening. And she was growing frustrated.

Her phone buzzed. A number she didn't recognize. She answered. A man's voice. "Agent Nolan?"

"Yep."

"This is Carl Kingston, Caitlin's father."

Dani had given her number out to the Kingston family members. She wondered why the father of the victim would be calling. "Yes, Mr. Kingston. How're you doing?"

"Not great. Didn't sleep last night. Just feel numb all over, you know. I still can't believe this is real."

"I'm sorry. I can't imagine it."

"Look, I won't take up much of your time. But I thought about something this morning. Not sure if it has anything at all to do with this but wanted to pass it along anyway. After the birthday party ended yesterday, Caitlin showed me a photo on her cell phone of one of the catering-crew guys who had handled the setup and teardown. She said Piper told her she thought she recognized the guy from the night when her mother was killed in the car accident last year."

"How do you mean?"

"I'm honestly not sure. Caitlin said Piper thought she remembered a guy being there right after the crash. Piper was kind of freaked out about the whole thing. My daughter wanted to know if I knew anything about the guy."

"Do you?"

"No, I don't. Didn't recall ever seeing him before. But my brother Steve was standing there with me when this happened and might know something."

"Why do you say that?"

"He acted like he might recognize the guy and said he'd look into it."

"Have you talked to Steve about it?"

"I tried calling him a few minutes ago but didn't get him. I doubt it's anything, but you said to reach out if we thought of anything, big or small."

"Correct. Do you happen to have the photo Caitlin shared with you?"

"Yes, I do. You want me to text it over?"

"Please."

"Sending now."

A few seconds later, Dani was staring at a guy probably in his twenties with a goatee who wore a black T-shirt, blue jeans, and cowboy boots. The photo showed him carrying a stack of folding chairs. He looked kind of rough around the edges.

"Caitlin really loved working for the FBI," Carl said, suddenly musing. "Every time we talked to her about it, she just lit up. She felt so certain it was her future."

"I'm sorry I didn't get a chance to know her personally. People are speaking highly of her around here today."

"Yeah." He sighed deeply. "Please let me know if this thing with the photo turns out to be anything."

"I will. Thank you again."

Carl hung up. Dani grabbed a small notepad from the table where she'd jotted down phone numbers for various Kingston family members last night. She found one for Steve Kingston and dialed him. It rang four times and then went to voice mail. She left a brief message asking him to call her back. Then she stared at the photo again. *Who are you? And why was Piper Slater freaking out about you?*

TWENTY-SIX

Eddie watched the local cable newscast with a small smile on his face while sitting on the couch, smoking a joint inside his mother's trailer. The old lady was out picking up some lunch from a nearby burger place. A news story had just broken about another person found shot and killed inside a house in South Austin. The police suspected it was at the hands of the same man whom they were searching for in connection with the death of Caitlin Kingston last night: Jake Slater. Eddie had no clue how the two deaths were connected, but he felt that the more heat put on someone else—and not on him—the better. He was beginning to think they just might be able to get away with this whole thing.

But they still had the problem with the girl. Her face had also been on TV. What the hell were they supposed to do with her? Eddie wanted to get rid of her ASAP. Maybe not kill her, but possibly drive her down south across the Mexico border and sell her off. Eddie knew certain people who were connected to that type of thing. She was a pretty young girl—he for sure knew he could make a lot of money. And from what he'd heard, a girl traded across the Mexico border never made it back to the United States. At least not alive. But his mother refused to budge on it. The old lady still felt like the girl was a critical trump card should they be forced into needing one.

Eddie heard his mother's car return outside. The old lady stepped inside the trailer carrying two small food bags with her. She tossed one over to him on the couch. There was grease from the burger and fries soaking through the bottom of the paper bag. Eddie was starving. He ripped it open and quickly tore into his cheeseburger.

"You seen this yet?" he asked his mother, nodding at the TV news.

"Yeah, I seen it," she acknowledged. The old lady was already pouring herself a new round of whiskey. "Makes me nervous."

"Why?"

"Who is this guy? He's a wild card. Why's he out there killing people?"

"Who cares?" Eddie replied. "Keeps the police off us."

"I don't know. Makes me uneasy."

"They pin it all on him, we're able to walk away."

"Maybe."

The old lady downed her whiskey and poured herself another. Eddie chomped into his cheeseburger, and it shot grease across his fingers. Grabbing the TV remote, he flipped the channel over to a football game. Dolphins and Packers. They both turned toward the door when they heard another car pull up right outside the trailer. They weren't expecting company. The old lady rushed over and peered through the blinds.

"It's Beth," his mother said.

Eddie cursed, stood. "What the hell is she doing here? She's supposed to stay away from us until this is over."

"I don't know. But she looks really upset."

His mother opened the door to the trailer and let her hysterically crying daughter inside. Eddie's sister was twenty-five and, in the words of his buddies, a real knockout. Long blonde hair and curvy in all the right places. He'd gotten into a lot of fistfights with friends over the years who had tried to make moves on his hot little sister. But she didn't look like a knockout right now. Beth was a mess. Her face was smeared with makeup from all the crying. This wasn't good.

"What the hell are you doing here?" Eddie asked.

"It's over." Beth sobbed, trying to catch her breath.

"What's over?" asked the old lady.

"He ended it," Beth said.

"What?" said his mother. "Why?"

She looked up at her mom, swallowed. "I, uh . . . I told him the truth."

Eddie erupted. "You did *what*?"

"I had no choice, Eddie. He already suspected something. He had a picture that was taken of you from yesterday. He was completely flipping out and demanding answers from me. Said if I didn't come clean, it was over. So I told him about what happened last year. About how I was trying to protect him."

"You stupid girl!" the old lady hissed. "Why would you do that?"

"Because I love him, Mom!"

Eddie was cursing up a storm. "He knows about last night?"

She looked over to him and reluctantly nodded.

Eddie threw his burger across the trailer. "This is unbelievable, Beth. We are so screwed!"

"I couldn't stop myself," Beth explained. "He was *so upset* with me! I'd never seen him like this before. He kept saying if we had any future together that I had to be completely honest with him."

"You are such an idiot," his mother said to Beth.

"Shut the hell up!" Beth yelled at her. "You don't even know what love is. Your man ran off to get the hell away from you."

Eddie could tell his mother was about to attack Beth physically, so he stepped in between them to try to defuse the situation. Fighting right now wasn't going to get them anywhere. But they were all screwed depending on what her man did next. Especially Eddie—he had blood all over his hands.

"So what's he going to do, Beth?" Eddie asked.

"I don't know," she admitted. "He looked so devastated. He kept blaming himself for everything and talking about how he had to come clean. To make this right. Then he wrote me a big-ass check and told me to get out of town as fast as possible. And not to tell anyone where

I was going. And that maybe after all of this finally calms down again, he'd come find me."

The old lady poured herself more whiskey and quickly downed it. "Does he know about the girl?"

She nodded. "But I swore to him she was OK, and I didn't know where you had her. I wanted to give you a chance to get out of here, too. Before he did something."

"OK, good," his mother said. She seemed to have calmed down. Eddie was unsure why. This whole thing was spiraling out of control.

"I'm sorry," Beth said. "I didn't want any of this to happen."

His mother put her hand on Beth's shoulder. "Hey, it's OK. We're all going to be OK. Just go back home, pack up some of your things, and then get back over here. We will all leave together, as a family."

Beth exhaled deeply, nodded, wiped the tears from her face with her fingers. Then she left. Eddie watched through the front window as his sister climbed back into her Honda Accord and drove off.

"So that's it?" Eddie said. "We're just going to leave?"

His mother's eyes grew narrow. "No, we're not leaving, son. You're going to go take care of this right now."

Eddie knew what she meant. "It will destroy Beth. She does love him."

"You think I care about her precious feelings right now? That guy comes clean, we're all going to prison. And I'll die in there."

"We can go to Mexico instead. Dad did it."

"I'm too old to live on the run. Plus, your daddy died two weeks after he crossed the border. Shot in an alley by a drug dealer."

Eddie's eyes widened. "What? You never told me that."

She shrugged. "You were still a kid who kept praying your daddy would come home. I didn't feel like it was something you should ever know."

Eddie cursed. "Well, you picked a real nice time to say something."

"Stop whining. Go make your daddy proud by doing what you have to do right now to take care of his family."

TWENTY-SEVEN

Logan Gervais smoked a cigarette while sitting in his black Taurus. He was parked on a hill overlooking the river with a great view of downtown spread out before him. The satellite radio was tuned to old-school jazz. John Coltrane currently filled up his speakers. Gervais loved the classics. In his opinion, *A Love Supreme* was one of the greatest jazz albums of all time. Living in New York City gave him access to the world's best up-and-coming jazz musicians. Gervais spent several nights a week out in the clubs. He could play a little saxophone himself but never quite had the ear to do much with it. If he got the opportunity, Gervais planned to visit the Elephant Room later tonight to listen to some jazz. He'd read some good things about the local club. A lot of the greats had played there.

But first things first. He needed to handle his business today.

Sitting there, waiting, Gervais was admittedly a little frustrated. He had not made as much progress tracking down his target as he'd hoped by this point in the day. All the appropriate players on the list for his target were being properly monitored. There were more than a hundred. Gervais had his laptop open in the passenger seat next to him. Several different digital boxes rotated on the screen, displaying various calls, emails, texts, and social media messages. Gervais had programmed a litany of key words that would trigger an alert for him. But nothing had come through yet. Either his target was operating completely alone, or he was communicating with someone who was not currently under Gervais's surveillance.

The football coach had done a good job staying off the radar thus far. But he couldn't hide forever. Eventually, he would reach out to someone who would come back to bite him. They always did. Gervais had never tracked anyone who stayed off the grid forever—it just took patience. So Gervais had been sitting there, enjoying his cigarettes, the view, and some soul-enriching jazz.

But finally, Gervais got an interesting hit.

His laptop dinged. Pulling it over, Gervais studied the screen. The alert came from the key words *Sarah Slater*. Gervais's eyes narrowed. An unidentified phone number had reached out to someone on his list by text message. The strand was peculiar and certainly put him on high alert. Someone was demanding a meeting and threatening the contact person if he didn't show up. Using his phone, Gervais pulled up the location mentioned in the text exchange. Alliance Children's Garden was in the heart of downtown and only five minutes away from him.

Setting his laptop aside, Gervais put the car in drive.

TWENTY-EIGHT

Jake sat in his truck, which was parked in a lot next to the Palmer Events Center downtown, and stared wide-eyed at the shocking breaking news he was just now reading on his burner phone. What the hell? Judd McGee was dead? Jake couldn't believe it. And the police suspected that Jake had shot and killed him early this morning? Why? How did this happen? Who would've shot him? Jake's head was spinning. Could it have been Judd's stepdaughter? Had the little girl pulled the trigger and then pinned it on Jake? That theory was so far-fetched, but he could come up with no other explanation as to why the man was dead only hours after Jake had accosted him.

One thing was clear. The police and media target placed squarely on Jake had just grown exponentially in size and scope. More photos of him were posted—most of them taken from various social media channels—and there was now a toll-free hotline set up by the police for people to call who spotted Jake in the city or had more information that led to his arrest. While he had been under the microscope before, Jake now felt like he had a thousand spotlights on him. But he couldn't go into hiding. He had to keep moving forward to find answers that would lead him to Piper. And that meant him walking into a public park right now.

Jake had no idea if Brent Grisham would actually show up at the location he'd indicated in his terse text earlier. The attorney had not responded to his threatening message. For all Jake knew, the guy could've already brushed off the whole thing as if it had originated from some random whack job. A man in his position with the governor might get a lot of nonsensical texts and emails and probably smartly ignored most of them. But Jake hoped the fact that he'd specifically mentioned Sarah by name would make the difference. There had clearly been *something* going on between the two of them when she'd died last year. An affair? Jake couldn't be 100 percent certain, but he had a bad feeling about it. But even if it was an affair, that was still a long way to murder. Either way, Jake knew he'd need to keep his cool to get the information he wanted. A difficult task was at hand no matter what direction this went—*if* Brent showed up.

Getting out of his truck, Jake walked down a maze of sidewalks that cut through wide-open fields of green grass. Alliance Children's Garden was set in the middle of beautiful Butler Metro Park, which hugged the downtown running trails along the river. Built next to a large pond, the children's garden was two acres of recreational space that included a variety of climbing and exploring apparatuses mixed among hills, bridges, and water fountains. Jake had been there several times with Piper when they just wanted to hang out together in a fun play space and goof off. Piper would run full speed in the plush grassy area and do as many back handsprings in a row as she could pull off. Her record was twelve—but that was before the crash last year. He thought about how difficult it had been for his daughter to get it back.

Jake woke, sat up in bed. What's that noise? Grunting? He looked over at the digital clock on his nightstand. Thirty minutes after midnight. He heard it again. More grunting. Piper? Jake got out of bed and moved to the bedroom window, which was cracked open. Piper was in the backyard, standing on the twenty-foot inflatable tumble track wearing shorts, a T-shirt, and her acro athletic shoes. Why was she out there right now? He watched as she bent down and then exploded upward, throwing her hands back, jumping off the ground, spinning backward, hands now tucked on her knees. She got three-quarters of the way around with her back tuck but couldn't stick the landing. She fell forward onto her knees and hands. "Dang it!" she yelled, clearly agitated.

Jake watched her for a couple of minutes. She tried again. Failed again. A third time. Another fall. Piper used to be able to easily nail her back tuck. But she had not been able to get it back yet with the loss of strength in her leg. Physical therapy was helping, but it had been slow. He knew his daughter was so frustrated. This was her joy. And it had been stolen from her this past year.

Grabbing a pair of jeans, Jake pulled them on and then walked out onto the back porch of his father's house. He could hear the crickets and see the stars in the sky. The stars had been one of the benefits of moving out of the city and to a country town. Although Piper had not seemed to be that impressed with them.

Piper went for it again. Another fall. This time she yelled, "I hate this!"

Jake moved down the steps and into the grass. Piper saw him for the first time.

"Sorry, didn't mean to wake you," she said.

It was humid, and she was sweating profusely.

"No, it's fine," he said. "Wasn't sleeping anyway. You're getting close."

"Liar," she said, frowning.

"Probably doesn't feel that way, but I can see it. Want a spot?"

"I guess." She sighed. "I may never get around without it."

Jakes stepped onto the tumble track and got on one knee. He put one hand at the small of her back. She didn't need much. Just a little support. He'd done this a thousand times over the years. He still remembered the first time she got her back handspring. She was eight. She ran around the backyard for five minutes in celebration.

"Just barely touch me," Piper said.

"I know. You got this."

With him spotting, Piper exploded upward, easily got around, and landed on her feet.

"See?" he said. "I barely did anything."

"Then why can't I get it on my own?"

"You will. But sometimes it helps to have Dad here."

"Well, you won't always be here for me."

"Yes, I will," he quickly responded.

He was surprised by how forcefully it came out. She looked back at him. They both seemed to be aware that he was talking about more than just spotting her.

"I will, Piper," he repeated. "Always. Let's go again."

Piper got into position. Jake placed his hand at her back. But he pulled it away at the last minute. She hit her back tuck completely on her own.

"I didn't touch you," Jake said, grinning.

She seemed shocked. "For real?"

"It was all you, baby. Don't think about it. Just do it again."

She got into position, jumped, spun, and nailed it again. This time she turned back with a huge smile on her face.

"Again," Jake said.

She did it again. Then a fourth time. And a fifth time. They were both beaming. Then she nearly jumped into his arms with more joy than he'd seen from her since before the accident. This was who they used to be. This was who he hoped they would be again.

"Always," Jake whispered.

Jake pushed that memory aside as he approached the garden area. It was Sunday, and the weather was decent—chilly but not unbearable—so the children's play spaces were busy with littles running and climbing all over while parents mostly sat on benches nearby. Jake hadn't given Brent any specifics on exactly where to meet here. That was intentional. Jake wanted to be able to survey the landscape without him being spotted first. Not that Brent should recognize him. Jake wore a USA baseball cap covering his hair and broke out a pair of sunglasses for the first time. He'd also put on a black hoodie with the Texas Tech logo on the front that he'd taken from the coaches' locker room. He wanted to keep mixing up his looks as much as possible in case the police or FBI had information about a particular outfit. He hadn't seen anything mentioning facial hair or wardrobes while reading the online news.

Jake also had a secondary reason for not giving Brent a specific meeting spot. He wanted to be able to monitor whether the attorney brought anyone with him. Would he show up alone? Or would he bring company? While the governor's chief of staff could've chosen to ignore Jake's text threats altogether, Brent could also be taking them very seriously. The prospect of dealing with a security detail would likely push Jake to abort and leave him back at ground zero.

Staying on the outskirts of the children's garden, Jake began to slowly circle the entire area and as casually as possible study all the people. Still no sign of Brent. He checked his watch. It was a few minutes after eleven already. This made him uneasy. If the guy didn't show up, what was next? He'd have to somehow hunt Brent down. That would not be an easy or quick task. Jake kept walking, watching the kids, examining the adults on the benches, feeling more panicked with each minute that clicked past eleven. Then he spotted the governor's chief of staff. Brent stood by a collection of water fountains that sporadically sprang up out of concrete where kids would play in their swimsuits during the summer. It was way too cold for kids to be in the water today. Brent was about Jake's height, clean-shaven, with slicked-back black hair. He wore a long black trench coat over what looked like a dark suit with a tie and black dress shoes. Brent was the epitome of a high-powered attorney. The man's eyes were on his phone, and he was typing something out.

Jake's burner phone suddenly buzzed.

I'm here. Now what?

Before approaching, Jake took a long look all around Brent, searching for any suspicious characters. He had images of Secret Service types standing at a distance with sunglasses on and wearing earpieces. But he didn't spot anyone who looked like that. Hopefully, Brent had come by himself. Taking a deep breath and letting it out slowly, Jake made his move. He circled the water-fountain area and stepped in closer to the man. When he did, Brent set his sights on him.

"Brent," Jake acknowledged in a tone that showed he knew the man.

The attorney's eyes grew narrow. "Who the hell are you?"

The fact that Brent didn't immediately recognize him was encouraging. His disguise had worked. Jake reached up and pulled off his sunglasses. He needed to quickly get information and get the hell out of there. He figured revealing his identity was the fastest way to do that.

Brent cursed. "Jake?"

"Stay calm, Brent. I just need information from you."

His mouth dropped open. "You're the most wanted man in Austin right now, Jake. There's a citywide police hunt going on for you. And you want me to stay calm?"

"None of it is true."

"Is that why we're here? You need a lawyer?"

"No, it's about Sarah."

Brent visibly swallowed. "What about her?"

"How long had the affair been going on?"

Brent pitched his head. "What affair?"

"Please don't make this harder on me than it already is. I saw the text messages between the two of you in the two days before her death last year. I know you were seeing each other. I also know you had eyes for my wife for a long time. So you can stop the damn act already. I don't have time for it."

"Why the hell are we having this conversation right now? Sarah has been gone for over a year, and you're on the run from the damn police. And your daughter is missing."

"I don't have time to explain." Jake stepped aggressively closer, got within a few feet of Brent. "I need the truth from you, Brent. Right now. My whole world has collapsed. Do you understand me?"

Brent put up a defensive hand. "All right, settle down. But it's not at all what you think. Look, it's true. I always had a thing for Sarah. I'm not going to lie. But we were *not* having an affair last year."

"But you were seeing each other secretly. I saw the texts."

"Yeah, I know. We were. But it was about something else. I swear."

"What was it about?"

"She needed legal advice about a work situation. That's all."

"You expect me to believe that? The night she died, you told her that you both needed to be careful, especially because of your job."

"It's complicated. I have attorney-client privilege and all. I really shouldn't be telling you any of this."

Jake felt anger surge within him. Brent had answers. He knew it. So he wasn't going to allow some legal technicality to put up a roadblock. He reached up with both hands and grabbed Brent's jacket in tight fists. "You think I give a damn about that? I swear, Brent, you better start spilling it. While I'm innocent in those other two deaths, I may have my first victim right here, right now, if you don't start talking."

Brent's eyes flared up. Jake could tell his message was getting across.

"Look, it was about one of her brothers, OK?"

"What? Which brother?"

"Steve."

"What about him?"

"Sarah had discovered that Steve had been stealing money from the family firm for years. I'm talking about millions of dollars that he'd been stashing away in offshore accounts. Sarah wasn't sure what to do about it, both from a legal and familial standpoint. That's why we were meeting. We were trying to figure it out. I swear, that's all."

Jake released his grip, took a step back. Steve? Embezzlement? He was stunned to hear that. Steve was the youngest of the brothers. He was kind of the black sheep of the family. Steve was never as smart or as academically accomplished as his two older brothers or his younger sister. According to Sarah, her father had to make significant donations to get Steve into Dartmouth but also to get him his finance degree. Because of this, Lars treated Steve differently from the others—like he was more of a nuisance. And Lars had never given him the same high-level company platforms as his siblings. Steve's relationship with his father was always strained. Still, Jake was surprised to hear that Steve was willing to steal money from the family. Steve feared his father. They all did.

"Did Steve know about Sarah's discovery?" Jake asked.

Brent shook his head. "I don't know. Sarah was going to speak with him. But I don't know if it ever happened. She died before I got the chance to talk to her about it again."

"What did you do with this information?"

Brent shrugged. "Nothing. The whole family was already crushed about Sarah. I didn't feel like it was my place to roll another grenade into the situation. So I just let it go and figured it would work itself out on its own."

Jake's mind was racing. "You ever tell *anyone* about it?"

"Not a soul, until now. I didn't want to complicate my life."

"Did Sarah tell anyone else?"

"I don't think so. But how could I know that for sure?"

Jake stood there silently, his mind spinning, trying to process this new information. Did Sarah confront Steve? Could Steve have actually done something to harm his own sister? Was his brother-in-law capable of such a horrible thing? Steve was passive. He was not overly aggressive like his father or his two brothers, who were all dominating figures. So it was difficult to imagine him making a dangerous move like that on his own sister.

Then again, Jake knew money and power could make people crazy.

TWENTY-NINE

Gervais stood behind a climbing wall at Alliance Children's Garden wearing a gray running suit and a black ski cap. His gun with silencer was tucked in his hidden waist holster. Across the way, he put eyes on his target for the very first time. With the baseball cap and goatee, the football coach looked different from the photos—but it was definitely him. His build was the same. He stood in front of the other man, who wore a black trench coat and dress shoes. Their conversation looked heated.

Gervais felt itchy to somehow isolate Slater and take his shot. But he didn't want to do it in the open—especially with all these kids running around. He'd wait to follow, looking for him to separate from others. Then he'd go for the kill. However, if the two men left the park together, Gervais might have to alter his approach. One way or another, he planned to finish this assignment right now.

Gervais looked over when a tour bus suddenly pulled to the curb near the park. He watched as a pack of what looked like tourists started filing out and began to head in his direction. Probably forty of them. Gervais cursed. This was not what he needed right now. He considered it for only a second before deciding to make his move. He was an expert marksman from a distance. If he was sudden and discreet, Gervais was certain he could pick off his target, put the gun away, and then hit the running trail nearby.

Just another jogger.

THIRTY

Brent said, "You have to turn yourself in, Jake. I mean, I work for the damn governor. I can help you through this. Let me."

Jake looked up. "Why would you even do that for me?"

"Because I really cared about Sarah. And I know she loved you."

"I can't," Jake said.

"Why? You're going to get yourself killed running around out here."

"I wish I could explain. It's just . . ."

Two little boys playing chase nearby suddenly bolted into their immediate area. One of the boys wasn't watching where he was going and slammed right into Jake's ankles with a serious thud. Jake reached down to help the boy up. When he did, Jake heard a loud but muffled *thump!* from somewhere behind him. Brent let out a sudden gasp, staggered backward. Jake's head whipped up. He stared at Brent, confused, and then watched as the man fell to the ground while clutching his throat. Jake could see blood pouring out of the man's neck. What the hell had just happened? Had someone shot him? Jake spun around, searching the area. But he didn't see anyone with a gun.

The two boys nearby suddenly screamed at the sight of Brent lying on the ground with blood everywhere. This made everyone turn to stare at them, which brought on more screams and more alarm. Jake felt eyes all over him. Did they think he'd done this to Brent? Would these people recognize him? He had to get out of there. Jake took off running. Then he heard the same sound as before—*thump!*—and felt a ricochet off a stone wall right beside him. Someone was shooting at him. He took another peek back but couldn't see anyone with a gun. Where the hell was the shooter? Had the bullet that hit Brent in the neck been meant for him? Had he been saved only by some random kid?

Jumping over a half-stone wall, Jake hit the ground on the other side and then cut through an artificial grass space loaded with kids' colorful playscapes. Jake wanted to get away from all the children as fast as possible. He didn't want any kids getting caught in the sudden cross fire. Darting across a small bridge, he heard another *thump!* and saw a spark of metal ignite from the bridge right in front of him. On instinct, Jake dived headfirst at the end of the bridge onto another sidewalk, rolled once, and then staggered to his feet again. He was finally away from the kids in the park and racing as fast as he could toward a heavily wooded ravine next to a railroad track. The tree coverage should help shield him. But he had no clue where to go to get away.

Running into the trees, Jake found himself engulfed by tall grass. This was not part of the well-landscaped park. The ravine was basically left untouched and in its natural state. He zigged and zagged around trees, keeping his head as low as possible, trying not to lose his balance. It became more difficult as the ground beneath him began to slope down toward the bottom of the ravine. The unkempt grass made it hard to see where he was stepping, and this caused him to catch a toe on a big rock and spill headfirst. He tumbled forward and then slid on his stomach in a muddy area for more than fifteen feet.

But he didn't stay down long—he quickly picked himself back up.

Jake looked behind him. Was he still being chased? He stayed very still, searching everywhere. And then a guy suddenly appeared. It was clear the guy didn't know exactly where Jake had gone. Jake squinted and took his first good look at the man. He was wearing a gray running suit and a black ski cap. Looked to be in his midthirties. He was certain he'd never seen the guy before. Could he be an off-duty police officer or FBI agent? But the fact that the guy had never even given him a chance to surrender—no *Stop! Hands up!*—and that he was using some kind of silencer on his gun to muffle the shots told him this was something altogether different. This guy wasn't trying to bring Jake into custody. The man was intent on killing him. Why? What was happening?

The guy in the running suit continued a slow path through the woods, searching over to Jake's left. Jake took a step back, wondering if he might be able to hide behind a cluster of trees. Maybe he could duck away, let the guy pass, and then Jake could rush back to the park. But the heavy grass area beneath him again proved disastrous. Jake stepped on a twig that cracked. He froze, looked up at the guy, who was about thirty yards over to his left. The guy in the ski cap spotted him, instantly raised his gun. Jake cursed, darted to his right. He heard two *thumps!* that splintered the tree right above him.

Ducking as low as possible, Jake raced down to the bottom of the ravine, intentionally cutting back and forth around as many trees as possible, trying desperately to guard himself from incoming bullets. He reached the bottom, skipped through a shallow creek, and then hit the hill on the other side. He dismissed any further ideas of finding a hiding spot. He needed to keep running. Jake could now hear sirens in the background. Someone had likely called the police about the man shot in the park. Jake hoped Brent would survive, but it didn't look good from his quick glance. The attorney had been bleeding badly from the neck and seemed to be gasping for his life. How had this gunman known Jake was meeting with Brent? Was he following the governor's chief of staff?

The climb up from the ravine was more challenging than the race down. Jake's legs were on fire with each step. Thankfully, there was even more tree coverage on his ascent. This time he chose not to look back, knowing that even a second lost in his escape could cost him his life.

He just kept darting in and out of trees, cutting left, then right, trying to keep himself from ever being a sitting duck. Above him, he suddenly heard an approaching cargo train. The train's bell was ringing, followed by the long wail of the loud horn. Jake had heard these same sounds for years while out on the practice fields over at Austin High, which was not far away. Jake wondered if he might be able to use the train to somehow escape the man with the gun below him.

Reaching the top of the hill, Jake watched as the front of the train— the locomotive—whizzed right past him down the tracks and headed out onto a train bridge that crossed over the river. Jake knew he couldn't second-guess himself. He ran straight up beside the train, looking for some way to jump onto one of the freight containers. The gravel that lined the tracks made it difficult for him to keep good traction. He nearly fell twice before regaining his balance. The train was moving at high velocity. Jake was quickly approaching the bridge. It was now or never. Jake figured he had one shot at this. If he jumped and missed, he might badly injure himself, or worse.

The yellow cargo containers had bars to open and shut the big sliding doors. He had to go for one of those bars. One more glance behind him to time it out. He was twenty feet from hitting the bridge and running out of room. *Three . . . two . . . one.* He jumped, reached. His left hand caught a bar, but his right hand missed. His shoes dragged on the gravel for a moment while he frantically tried to reach back up with his right. A column for the bridge was about to hit him. Using every bit of strength in his left arm, Jake pulled himself back up and finally got his right hand onto the same bar. Then he snuggled in as close as possible as his container raced out onto the bridge over the water.

Jake spun his head around, peered behind him. The guy with the gun appeared beside the tracks just as the caboose of the train sped past him. The train was going too fast for the man to catch up to it. And Jake was already too far away for the guy to get a good shot at him.

He'd survived—but barely.

THIRTY-ONE

Jake hopped off the cargo train once it slowed to pull into a Central Austin loading station. Then he hustled on foot back through the city until he finally returned to his truck parked next to the Palmer Events Center. From a distance, he could see the chaotic scene over at the Alliance Children's Garden. Police and emergency vehicles were spread all over the place, and a big crowd of onlookers had gathered where Jake had stood talking with Brent about twenty minutes ago. Was Brent dead? Had the bullet taken the man's life? Jake had no plans to get close enough to the scene to find out. But the thought that the man might be dead because he'd shown up to meet with Jake was tough to swallow. Everywhere Jake went right now resulted in more dead bodies.

First, Judd McGee. Now, Brent Grisham.

Why? What was going on? How was this all connected?

Jake decided he had no choice but to toss his new burner phone. If the text exchange he'd had with Brent might somehow be traced back to him, Jake couldn't chance leaving himself open to that kind of exposure. But having no line of potential communication with Piper or her captors left him feeling severely anxious again. He had kept a small sliver of hope alive that Piper might suddenly be released and would call him on the phone. That hope was now dead.

All this had to somehow relate to Sarah's discovery that her brother was stealing millions from the family firm. But would Steve really go to such lengths to cover up his crime? Would he have his own sister killed? His niece Caitlin too? And then have Piper kidnapped? It was hard to fathom, even with Steve's personal and marital issues. Steve and his wife, Brooke, fought a lot and had embarrassed themselves plenty of times at family functions. When they were unable to have kids, Brooke seemed to turn on him. They'd done medical testing and discovered Steve was infertile. This had been yet another factor that had put Steve in a weak position with his overbearing father, who clearly obsessed over having a brood of grandchildren. Brooke also seemed to despise him for it. But they never divorced, probably because of pressure from both wealthy families. Stability protected money and power, according to Lars. Which Jake found ironic since he knew Lars had secretly encouraged Sarah to divorce him numerous times and move on.

Pulling away from the parking lot, Jake drove out of downtown proper and into the exclusive suburb of Westlake. He was headed straight to Steve's house to confront the man directly. He could feel his anger surging with the thought that his brother-in-law might be behind Piper's abduction. Like everyone else in the family, Steve lived in an exquisite place near downtown. Jake wondered if he would actually be home. He figured most of the Kingston family might be gathered over at his in-laws' estate today. No doubt his father-in-law would be blaming him for everything that had happened while not realizing it was probably his own son who had caused this devastation.

Jake slowed as he pulled down a street of luxury homes in a neighborhood called Rollingwood until he came upon a private cul-de-sac. Steve's house was a super-modern two-story with floor-to-ceiling windows that looked out over a heavily wooded area. Jake parked up the street away from the house. He quickly changed out of the black hoodie he was wearing—it had mud all down the front—and put on the dark-gray cotton jacket. He also swapped out his baseball cap for the ski cap again. Getting out, Jake briskly walked toward the cul-de-sac. He kept his eyes down on the sidewalk as a neighbor pulled out of a garage in a Cadillac Escalade and drove on past him. How long could he keep this up? Every time someone gave him a second look, it sent shivers down his spine. His nerves felt completely shot. But he knew the answer—he had to keep going until he finally had Piper safely back in his arms.

Jake's initial plan was to go straight up to the front door and just bang on it. When Steve answered, he'd make a bold maneuver inside and abruptly address his brother-in-law before the man could make any sudden moves. Jake was much bigger and stronger than Steve. Unless his brother-in-law had a gun on him, Jake knew he could physically manhandle him. But when he got to the glass front door, he found it cracked open two feet. Why? Then Jake looked through the glass and spotted a vase of flowers shattered on the hardwood floor right next to an entry table. He squinted. Next to the vase were red streaks on the floor that led down a hallway. Jake moved inside the house, listened. He could hear a TV on down the same hallway. Sounded like a football game. Was it coming from Steve's office? Jake knew the house well. He'd come here often over the years. He knelt, closely examined the red streaks, quietly cursed. Blood. He looked back at the broken vase on the floor and at the front door left open. Whose blood? What had happened? And what was he about to discover?

Jake moved cautiously down the hallway toward Steve's office. While he could hear the TV announcers, Jake heard nothing else in the house. Except maybe the beating of his own heart in his chest. He passed a guest bathroom on his left and then a hallway that he knew led to bedrooms in the back of the house. But the red streaks on the floor continued to the corner office. Jake stepped inside the office with trepidation. He cursed again. Steve was lying facedown on the hardwood floor behind his desk with both of his arms spread out in front of him. His brother-in-law wasn't moving. Blood was pooling up all around his body. Jake raced over to Steve, pulled on his shoulder to turn him over.

The man was limp. The front of his brother-in-law's white polo shirt was soaked in red and completely mangled. Steve was dead. Someone had shot him. Was that someone still here? Jake felt panic grip him. This was not at all what he'd expected to find when he got here.

If Steve was the person behind all this, why was he dead? Why had someone killed him? Jake had to get out of there. He stood but then glanced down at the desktop, which was covered in various files and paperwork. He began rummaging through all the material just to see if he could find anything that might be connected to his situation. Most of it looked like standard investment printouts and spreadsheets. Then he spotted a checkbook beneath one of the papers. Grabbing it, Jake opened it and began scanning the carbon copy receipts. He stopped and stared wide-eyed at the last check written in the book. It was dated today, for $50,000, and made out to someone named Beth Spiller. It had to be the same Beth mentioned in the phone call he'd overheard last night. Fifty thousand dollars? That was a hell of a lot of money. Who was she? Eddie Cowens had mentioned on the phone call from Piper's phone something about Beth and her boss. Could Beth work for Steve at Kingston Financial?

Jake froze when he heard movement from somewhere else in the house. It sounded like the bumping of a chair on the hardwood floor. Then a man cursed.

THIRTY-TWO

Dani parked on the curb outside Steve Kingston's house. She dialed his phone number and again listened to his voice mail greeting. He had not responded to any of her urgent messages, so she'd decided to try to track him down. She wanted to get more information about the unidentified man in the photo that Carl Kingston had texted over to her. Getting out of her vehicle, she walked up the path toward the front door. That's when she noticed the glass door was pushed open. A piece of black duct tape covered the doorbell security camera. Peering inside, she noticed a broken vase of flowers on the floor in the foyer along with red streaks on the floor. She felt her adrenaline spike. She recognized the red streaks and immediately pulled out her gun. Stepping inside the home, Dani paused to listen. She could hear a TV on somewhere in the house. It sounded like it was coming from a hallway to her right—the same direction as the blood streaks on the floor.

"Hello? Anyone home?" Dani called out. Even with her suspicions, she wanted to be careful to not enter a home uninvited and get herself into trouble. "Mr. Kingston, this is Special Agent Dani Nolan with the FBI. May we talk for a moment?"

She stood there a second and listened. No response. She glanced over and took in the impressive windows in the main living room that looked out over a pool. There was no one outside on the back patio. Then she began to step down the hallway toward where she could hear the TV, careful to avoid the blood on the floor.

She paused outside the room with the TV. "Hello? Mr. Kingston?"

Still no response. She turned the corner, gun ready. That's when she saw Steve on his back on the floor with blood everywhere. His eyes were open but glazed over. She guessed he'd been shot multiple times in the chest. Someone had dragged him into this room. How long ago? Based on the pooling of the blood, she presumed it had just happened. Was the shooter still in the house? Dani rushed out of the office and into the hallway. She began searching one room at a time, making sharp motions, gun prepared to fire. She quickly cleared a section of bedrooms and bathrooms in the back corner of the house. But then she suddenly heard a door open and shut in the main living room.

Darting back to the living room, Dani paused at the hallway corner, took a quick peek, but spotted no one. She was certain she'd heard a door. But it wasn't the front door. She was sure of that. A back patio door? Gun aimed, she peeled off the corner and entered the living room, her eyes searching everywhere. Two patio doors led out to the pool. Dani noted that one of them was unlocked. She opened the door, stepped out onto the back patio. There was a dining table and sectional sofa in front of a built-in fireplace. A black metal railing secured the area around the pool, which looked to drop off significantly into a yard somewhere below. Dani scooted around the outdoor furniture and made her way over to the metal railing. She could see nothing in the grass and woods beyond the yard. But then she heard movement behind her.

Spinning around, Dani came face-to-face with a man with a gun aimed straight at her at about twenty feet away. He was probably in his twenties with a goatee, wearing blue jeans, cowboy boots, and a black leather jacket. She recognized him. He was the same guy from the photo that Carl Kingston had sent over to her earlier. The guy who had Piper freaking out at the birthday party yesterday. Dani kept her gun down, trying to keep herself from being shot. But the look on the guy's face told her he was going to pull the trigger anyway. Before he did, someone else suddenly appeared from a patio door, rushed the guy, and put his shoulder right into him. Together, the two of them crashed into the metal railing and flipped over it before falling into the yard about ten feet below. Dani raced to the metal railing herself and stared down. The man in the cowboy boots was already scrambling off toward the woods. The other guy who'd tackled him seemed dazed by the fall as he tried to get himself up off the ground.

Dani raised her gun, aimed it down at the guy who'd just saved her life.

"Don't move!" she commanded.

The man looked up at her.

"Jake?" she said.

THIRTY-THREE

Jake froze. Behind him, the intruder was already disappearing some-where deeper into the woods. The last few minutes had been a blur. After hearing a noise in the house earlier and a man cursing, Jake had cautiously searched. But his searching had been interrupted by Dani's sudden and unexpected entrance into the house. Jake had hidden in the media room on the opposite side of the kitchen, waiting for an oppor-tunity to get away. He didn't want Dani or the FBI thinking he had something to do with Steve's death. The police were already wrongfully pinning other deaths on him.

Then Jake heard the opening and shutting of a back patio door. He'd carefully crept into the kitchen to get a better look. He couldn't see anyone at first. When Dani appeared in the living room, he hid behind the kitchen island. He again heard the back patio door open. Jake slipped through the kitchen toward the front door. He was ready to bolt when he took one last peek out to the back patio. First, he'd spotted Dani looking out toward the woods. Then he noticed a man he recognized as Eddie Cowens from the photograph he'd found in the trailer earlier suddenly appear behind her with a gun in his hand. Jake had every opportunity to just run away. To dart out the front door and protect himself. But he couldn't do that. He'd responded on instinct instead. And now he was staring up at Dani, who had her gun aimed directly at him and seemed ready to pull the trigger—unlike their last encounter in the alley.

"Hey, Dani. Been a long time."

That's all he could think to say in this surreal moment. He was staring at a woman who'd once held his heart. A woman he probably should've married. Would this same woman now take him down with a bullet?

"Jake . . . why're you here?"

"Probably the same reason as you. Searching for answers."

Dani moved closer to the metal railing, her gun still pointed at him. "Steve Kingston is dead."

"I know."

Her forehead wrinkled. "Did you . . . ?"

"No, of course not. I'm guessing it was the guy who just got away."

"Do you know who he is?"

"The same man who took my daughter and is holding her captive somewhere."

Her forehead bunched. "How do you know that?"

"It's complicated. You need to put your gun down."

She held it even firmer. "I can't, Jake. I have a job to do."

"I'm innocent, Dani. You have to believe me."

"I *do* believe you."

He tilted his head. "You do?"

"Yes. But you have to turn yourself in right now so I can actually help you."

"I can't do that."

"Why the hell not?"

"I don't have time. They may kill her. You just have to trust me."

"I'm trying to save your life, Jake. Someone has hired a professional hit man to take you out. It's not just the police out there hunting for you."

Jake tilted his head. A hit man? It had to be the same guy from the park earlier. Who would've hired a hit man to kill him? Was it Steve? But why would he have done that when Jake was already in serious trouble with the police and the FBI?

"Who wants you dead, Jake?" Dani asked.

"I don't know. But I have to go now."

Jake wanted to tell Dani the truth. He desperately wanted help. He felt so alone in all this. But it scared him to get the FBI involved at this point. He believed he was close to the truth, and it would lead him straight to Piper. So he had to risk being shot. He turned to leave, but Dani yelled at him.

"Jake! Don't move, or I'll have no choice but to shoot you!"

But Jake didn't turn back. Instead, he raced off into the woods.

Dani never pulled the trigger.

THIRTY-FOUR

Twenty minutes after letting Jake go, Dani stood in the living room of Steve Kingston's house surrounded by a swarm of police and other emergency personnel who were all working the crime scene. Her boss, Simon, stood in front of her, arms crossed, looking more pissed off than she'd ever seen him. She'd had no choice but to admit her reluctance to take down Jake, as he'd ordered, because a security camera on the back patio had captured the entire event. Dani was still reeling from what had happened and the confusing conversation she'd had with Jake. Why wouldn't he tell her what was going on? Who was the other guy who'd nearly shot her on the patio? So many unanswered questions were ping-ponging in her head. But the scowl currently on Simon's face told her she was not going to get the chance to go after the answers.

"I have no choice but to suspend you, Dani," he said. "You know that, right?"

"Jake Slater is innocent. How do you expect me to shoot a man who'd just saved my life?"

"You can't say that for sure. How do you know the other guy shot Steve Kingston? It could've been Slater. Or they could've been working together. We don't have that part on camera. You've gotten yourself too emotionally invested. You're not thinking clearly."

"If they were working together, why would Jake have tackled that guy?"

"I don't know. But I have a real mess on my hands now. I can't keep you on this case anymore. The media is already going to crucify me. Mitchell will take over from here."

Dani wanted to argue. She was getting close. She could feel it. But she knew fighting with Simon about this right now would get her nowhere fast.

"Do what you have to do, Simon."

"Look, just take the afternoon off, and go clear your head."

Dani left without another word. But she had no intention of taking the afternoon off. Jake had saved her life, and she wasn't going to leave him hanging out there on his own. Even if it jeopardized her job. Dani's phone buzzed as she was getting into her car. It was the old FBI friend she'd reached out to earlier who had retired to the Bahamas. Jester Bannon. He was a veteran agent who had taken her under his wing her first few years in DC.

"I got him," Jester said.

"The pilot?"

"Yep. Name's Marcus Jett. You believe that? A pilot with the last name *Jett*. Anyway, I tracked him down at a beach bar while he waited for his next client's flight."

"What did he say?"

"Said he had no idea who his passenger from New Jersey was this morning. His paperwork listed him as Jerry Tupoli. The passenger didn't say much and didn't want any help with his items. So the pilot just left him alone. But he did have the client who chartered the plane on his paperwork. Wyatt, Banks, and McKenzie. I already looked it up for you. A large corporate law firm in Austin."

A law firm? That could mean a lot of things. "Anything else?"

"Nah, that's it. I bought the pilot a couple of beers, and he happily shared."

"I really appreciate this, Jester. I owe you. How's the fishing down there?"

"Glorious. You should come visit."

"I will. Soon."

Dani hung up and immediately started searching the law firm on her phone. She pulled up the firm's fancy website and began scrolling through attorney profile pages. She didn't have to look very far to find a match for the gray-haired man who had been in the airport hangar with Logan Gervais earlier. Nelson Wyatt. He was a name partner. She did an individual search for Nelson Wyatt. He was clearly a hotshot attorney. There were dozens of stories and photos of Wyatt involved with big cases for high-profile corporate clients. She doubted Wyatt had hired a professional hit man for his own personal reasons. He had to have done it for a client. So which one? And why? She wondered if she could get her hands on a client list. Unlikely. She'd have to go straight to the source and see what, if anything, she could stir up.

Dani called up FBI headquarters and got patched through to a member on her team.

"I need you to get me an address ASAP. Nelson Wyatt."

Minutes later, she had it. The pin on her map app told her Nelson Wyatt lived only two miles away from Steve's house. All the rich people lived around this part of town. Dani started her Mazda and took off. She was pulling up to a massive house sitting along Lake Austin about five minutes later. Before she had a chance to knock on the front door and introduce herself, she spotted the same white Range Rover she'd seen parked in the airport hangar security video earlier pulling out of the driveway. Nelson Wyatt was behind the steering wheel. And he was in a hurry.

Dani did a quick U-turn and followed. She tried to strategize how to approach the man to get the necessary information out of him. Threats would likely get her nowhere. Men like Wyatt made careers out of legally keeping secrets for wealthy clients.

She followed the Range Rover into Zilker Park and trailed at a distance until he finally came to a stop in a small empty parking lot near the sand volleyball courts. Dani pulled off the park road and watched from a distance for a moment. Was he going for a run on the nearby trails? The lawyer just sat in his car and waited. She got her answer two minutes later when a sleek black Bentley pulled into the same parking lot and parked right next to the Range Rover. Wyatt climbed out of his vehicle. Dani cursed when the driver of the other vehicle also got out. Lars Kingston.

She watched as the two men huddled closely together and began engaging in an animated conversation. Dani's mind began racing. Could Lars have hired Logan Gervais? He had to be involved. It was too much of a coincidence for these two men to be meeting privately today unless it was connected to Gervais. But why? While Lars clearly disliked his former son-in-law, why would he hire a hit man to kill him under these crazy circumstances? Was he convinced Jake had killed his granddaughter last night and simply taking matters into his own hands? Powerful and wealthy people often played by their own rules.

THIRTY-FIVE

Jake sat in his truck and tried to regroup somehow from his encounter with both Eddie Cowens and Dani after finding his brother-in-law Steve shot dead in his office. Eddie must have been the one who'd shot him. Why? Jake had been working under the presumption that Steve was behind everything that had happened to Sarah and Piper. Was he wrong? Or was he right, and things had somehow gone sideways between Steve and Eddie?

Jake looked down and noticed that his fingers were trembling. He couldn't squelch the growing fear inside that—because of his encounter at Steve's house—Eddie might panic and make a devastating move with Piper. Their words from the phone call last night about what they'd do to Piper if police got too close echoed in his mind: *Then we do what we gotta do with her.* Was Eddie now going to head straight back to wherever they had Piper and kill her? Was she already dead? Maybe he should've told Dani the truth. Maybe she could've somehow stepped in and done something to find Piper. But he was terrified that telling Dani the truth would somehow backfire on him.

Jake thought about Beth Spiller, the name he'd found in Steve's checkbook. He had to find her. Because he'd tossed his burner phone, he had no current access to the internet to search for her. Jake still had

Sarah's old day planner with him, which listed her security codes for the offices of Kingston Financial. It was Sunday afternoon. The office was probably empty. Could he possibly find contact information for Beth Spiller inside the office?

Starting up the truck, Jake drove into downtown proper and found an open parking spot near 600 Congress, a high-rise office building in the heart of Austin's financial district. Kingston Financial occupied the entire thirtieth floor. Sarah's mother had decorated the office, and it dripped with the same rich luxury of their personal residence. An international design magazine had even run a feature on the office space a few years ago. Jake put the fake black-rimmed glasses back on, along with the gray cotton jacket and brown ski cap. Then he got out of the truck, took a few quick glances around for any signs of police, and headed straight up the sidewalk for the glass front doors of the building. He entered the spacious lobby, which was mostly empty. Two security guards sat behind a booth over to his right. Jake moved straight for the elevators, trying to look purposeful, like he belonged, and it was normal for him to stop by the office on a Sunday. Out of his peripheral vision, he could feel one of the security guards' eyes on him. Was it just casual monitoring like the guard would do with anyone who came to the building? Or was it more?

Jake didn't hang around to find out. Moving into the elevator corridor, he pressed a button, and one of the doors immediately opened. Rushing inside, Jake quickly punched the button for the thirtieth floor. But before the doors fully shut, someone else reached the elevator and stuck a hand in to block it. A fortysomething man in black slacks and a white dress shirt entered. He gave a quick nod at Jake, turned, and pressed the button for the twenty-fourth floor. The doors shut, and the elevator started to ascend.

"You work for Kingston Financial?" the guy asked. He was staring at Jake in the mirrored reflection of the elevator doors.

"What's that?" Jake asked, buying time to sort out a good answer.

The guy nodded at the elevator buttons. "Noticed you're headed up to the Kingston floor. I know a lot of the guys who work there."

"Oh, yeah. Uh, just started there last week."

"I didn't think they were hiring right now. Which section?"

Jake had no idea how to address that. "Foreign investments."

The guy gave him an odd look. "Gotcha."

Jake stared down at his hands, avoiding eye contact. He hoped that answer was sufficient because that was all he could come up with in the moment. The elevator stopped on the twenty-fourth floor.

"Well, tell Andy Reyes I said hey," the guy said, before exiting.

"Will do. Have a good one."

Jake had no idea who Andy Reyes was. But he was glad to get rid of that guy. The less interaction he had right now, the better. He just wanted to get in and out of Kingston Financial as quickly as possible. When the doors opened on the thirtieth floor, Jake eased out into the hallway. The glass doors of Kingston Financial stood in front of him. On the wall beside the doors was both a card-key scanner and a keypad. Jake pulled the piece of scrap paper where he'd written down Sarah's office code from his front pocket. Would the firm have canceled her security access after she'd died? Jake reached up, carefully typed in the six-digit code from the paper. He exhaled when a little red light on the keypad shifted to green. Reaching over, he pulled on one of the glass doors. It swung open easily, with no alarms going off. He was inside a moment later.

The name of the firm was emboldened from behind in bright lights on a white stone wall in front of him. There was a luxurious sitting area to his left with numerous leather sofas and chairs. The reception-ist station currently sat empty. Jake stepped into the lobby, paused to listen. He didn't hear anything from the various hallways. If someone was working this Sunday, they were deeper in the bowels of the office. Jake quickly stepped behind the reception counter and began looking around for a company contact list. He found a laminated list sitting under a keyboard by the computer. He ran his finger down the list searching for Beth Spiller. Bingo. He found her. Administrative assistant, special events. Beside her name was a phone extension. Picking up the reception phone, Jake pressed the extension and then listened. A phone began to ring down one of the hallways. Setting the phone on the counter without hanging up, Jake rushed down the hallway while trying to find the location of the ring. There were nice offices on the outside of the hallway and cubicles on the inside. The ringing was coming from one of the cubicles. But it stopped before he could locate the exact one. Hurrying back to the reception counter, he did the same exercise and again raced back down the hallway.

This time, he found the right cubicle before the ringing stopped. There was an L-shaped computer station with a short stack of metal bookshelves and a couple of short file cabinets. Jake sat in the desk chair, began searching the desktop. He immediately spotted a photo of a very attractive young blonde woman in a frame on the desktop. Was that Beth? She was squeezed in next to another young woman at a restaurant somewhere.

But it was another photo frame right next to it that really got his attention. There were two pictures in separate slots. The left picture was of two young kids, a girl and a boy, both wearing matching Christmas pajamas. The young girl was clearly Beth as a child. The picture on the right was present-day Beth with her arm wrapped around a guy who Jake was certain was Eddie Cowens. Jake's eyes went back and forth between the two pictures. Eddie was definitely the young boy in the picture on the left. Beth and Eddie must be brother and sister, even though they didn't share the same last name.

Jake began opening desk drawers to see if he could find Beth's address listed on anything. The first two drawers were nothing but office supplies. But the second drawer also contained something that made him pause. A small strip of photos taken at a photo booth somewhere. Beth was in the booth with Steve Kingston. And the fact that they were kissing on the lips in the bottom shot told him everything he needed to know. Steve was having an affair with Beth. That was the connecting point. Had Steve gotten Beth's brother to eliminate his potential exposure for stealing millions from the company? Or were Beth and her brother acting independently from Steve? The fact that Steve was now dead left him thinking the latter—but then why would Steve write a $50,000 check to Beth on the same day he was killed?

Jake had to find Beth. That was the way forward. He kept searching desk drawers. He found what he needed in the bottom drawer. Beth had a stack of opened personal mail. Her address was listed on a utility bill. He quickly shoved the bill in his pocket, along with the strip of photos, and headed back up the hallway. When he returned to the office lobby, he was startled to find one of the security guards from downstairs standing there. What was he doing? Had the guy from the elevator called down? Or was this just a random check-in? Jake tried to play it cool even though his heart was hammering away.

"Hey, how're you doing?" Jake said.

"Good. You?"

"Great. Can I help you with something?"

"Do you work here, sir?"

"Of course. Why else would I be here?"

"Right. It's just we got a concerned call about this floor."

"Concerned? Everything seems fine up here. No issues."

Jake kept racking his brain on the best way to get rid of this guy as soon as possible. He hadn't come all this way only to get apprehended by a security guard. But the guy did have a gun at his hip, which made Jake uneasy.

"Do you have ID on you, sir?" the guard asked.

"No, I left it in the car. Besides, I'm leaving anyway."

Jake decided to make a casual move around the guy, hoping he might just let him slip past without further incident. It didn't work.

"Hold up just a second, sir," the guard said, putting a hand out in front of Jake. "I just need to get your name, as a formality."

"Sure. Todd Hendricks."

The guard lifted a handheld radio to his mouth. "Can you run a check for me? Hendricks. Todd Hendricks. For Kingston, thirtieth floor."

Jake felt his adrenaline pumping. There was no chance the name was going to show up on whatever check they were running. Todd Hendricks was the name of a guy Jake had coached with early on in his career.

"Is this really necessary?" Jake said to the guard. "I'm leaving, and you can clearly see I have nothing with me."

"It will just be another minute, sir."

Jake was cursing inside. This was bad.

A guard on the other end of the radio replied. "No Todd Hendricks on the list."

The guard tilted his head at Jake.

Jake shrugged. "I just started last week."

The guard's eyes grew narrower. "OK, then let's just ride down together and get this sorted out in the lobby."

"Sure thing."

But Jake had no intention of going down to the lobby and huddling up with the security guards. There was no chance that would turn out in his favor. He had to get away from this guy and somehow get out of the building. The guard held the glass door of the office open for Jake to enter the hallway by the elevators. Passing by the guard, Jake lunged at him and shoved the guard as hard as he could. The man stumbled backward and collided with a tall potted plant before losing his balance and toppling over onto the floor. Jake darted for the door to the stairs. He obviously couldn't get into an elevator right now. As the door shut behind him, Jake could hear the guy shouting into his radio. *Black glasses . . . gray jacket . . . brown ski cap . . . gray goatee.*

Jake began bounding down two and three steps at a time. He was about ten flights down when he began to wonder what he was going to do when he encountered another security guard. They obviously knew he was in the stairwell. Should he peel off somewhere and hide? But he couldn't do that. They might call in the real police to come search for him. Jake had just assaulted the other security guard. He had to keep going.

Thinking quickly, Jake pulled off the gray cotton jacket, the ski cap, and the fake glasses. Then he reached up to his face, found a small corner of the fake gray goatee, and began ripping it from his face. Without using the adhesive removal, it hurt like hell. But he had no choice. He had to alter his appearance right now. A couple of more yanks and rips, and the fake hair was completely off. Jake patted his face to make sure it was all gone. He hoped his skin was not so red that it stood out. He opened the door to the elevator corridor on the eighteenth floor, tossed the items inside, and got to moving down the stairs again.

As expected, he heard the pitter-patter of feet racing up in the stairwell as he neared the twelfth floor. He also heard the opening and shutting of stairwell doors. The second security guard was likely making quick checks inside the elevator corridors of each floor. Jake took several deep breaths, trying to catch his wind, so he could bluff his way through this. He couldn't be panting when he faced the guard. With the bottom of his maroon T-shirt, he dabbed at his forehead to wipe away any excess sweat. He closed his eyes, said a quick prayer, and took one more deep breath. And then he calmly walked down the stairs until he came upon the buff security guard who was hurrying up in the opposite direction.

"Everything OK?" Jake asked, trying to hide the tremble in his voice.

The guard paused, examined him closely. "Looking for someone. Have you seen anyone else in this stairwell?"

Jake pointed behind him. "Yeah, just saw a guy just a second ago. He was in a hurry. Nearly knocked me over. I think he exited on the nineteenth floor."

"Nineteenth?"

"Yeah, pretty sure."

"All right, thanks."

"You bet. Good luck."

Jake stepped around the guard. He heard the guy lift his radio and tell his partner to check the nineteenth floor. Jake made sure to keep his steps steady for a few flights. But the closer he got to the ground floor, the faster his legs wanted to move. He finally reached the bottom. He pushed the door open and again steadied his pace so as to not draw any eyeballs. There were no security guards around the booth right now. Exiting the building, Jake stepped out onto the sidewalk along Congress Avenue.

Then he ran like hell.

THIRTY-SIX

Logan Gervais sat at the bar in the Four Seasons, sipping on a glass of bourbon and trying to soothe some of his frustrations over missing the opportunity to take out his target earlier in the public park. The football coach was surprisingly shifty, or maybe just damn lucky. There was no other explanation for how he'd somehow sidestepped every bullet the great ghost had offered up in his direction. And to catch a running train like that? And now this situation had turned into a much bigger mess for Gervais because one of his bullets caught the other man—who just happened to be the Texas governor's chief of staff. The man had died, and the media story was big. Gervais was watching it all unfold on the TV behind the bar. *Police are searching for the shooter . . . shooter still at large . . . eyewitnesses giving detailed reports of the incident.*

Gervais cursed. What a headache. He was not overly concerned about being identified. He had been very discreet with each attempted shot. It just created theatrics he'd rather not have to deal with while trying to complete this assignment by the end of the day. Gervais looked down at his laptop on the bar. An unexpected message from his client appeared in his in-box on his secured website. His eyes narrowed. A second assignment request. Three new targets in addition to the football coach. An older woman, along with a younger man and woman who were probably both in their twenties. Then an add-on about the recovery of a child who was in their custody. There was also a photo of the child, who looked to be in her early teens.

Gervais replied to the message.

Negative. This falls outside my normal scope.

He got a quick reply. Money is no object.
Gervais smiled. He'd played that well. Triple my fee.

Done. Please handle promptly.

Gervais quickly downed the rest of the bourbon and gathered his belongings.

THIRTY-SEVEN

Eddie spun the big tires on his truck as he entered his mother's trailer park at rapid speed. Dust and dirt kicked out and sprayed a man out walking his dog. But Eddie didn't give a damn. He was in a hurry to get the old lady and get the hell out of town as soon as possible. He knew they were in serious jeopardy after what had happened with the man and the woman at Steve Kingston's house. He couldn't stop cursing up a storm.

After taking care of Steve, Eddie could've easily just left the house. But he didn't. He decided to hang around and search for valuables inside the home. Eddie was in the master bathroom, sorting through women's jewelry in an elaborate jewelry box when he'd first heard someone else enter the house. Eddie hid away in the closet, waiting for the coast to clear. But then another person entered the property. A damn FBI agent. Eddie would've taken her out if not for the other guy unexpectedly interrupting him. Eddie's shoulder was killing him. The fall from the balcony had probably broken a bone or something. But he didn't have time to go to a doctor. He would take care of it later when they were free and clear of Austin.

Eddie had called his mother and told her to be ready to bolt. They were leaving town. He made a quick stop at his trailer and threw a bag of clothes together and then headed to the trailer park. He skidded the truck to a stop outside the old lady's trailer. Then he jumped out of the truck. The pretty young girl next door was outside again. But Eddie didn't even give her a second look. His heart felt like it was pumping a hundred miles an hour. Eddie had never shot a man up close like that before—that young woman last night had just been an accident. It was not a pleasant sight or feeling. He'd nearly thrown up all over the hardwood floor.

He again thought about the FBI agent. Had she gotten a good look at his face? He had duct-taped the front doorbell camera before taking care of Steve Kingston. But were there back patio cameras? Didn't matter. They were leaving and not looking back. He gave his mother no choice—they were going to Mexico. Eddie planned to be across the border before midnight tonight.

Eddie didn't bother knocking. He just swung the trailer door open. The old lady was scrambling to pack her things in a suitcase.

"We have to go, right now!" Eddie yelled.

"I'm not ready yet!"

"Damn it, Mom, we don't have time. Get in the truck!"

"What about Beth?"

"She's going to meet us over at the barn. We'll leave together from there."

"You tell her about Steve?"

"No. She'll fall apart. I'll tell her later, when we're on the road."

Eddie walked over to the window, peeked through the blinds. He wanted to make sure no police cars were suddenly showing up. He turned back around. His mother was still sorting through a dresser of clothes.

"Mom . . . now!"

"What about all my picture albums?"

"Leave them. The police ain't going to let you take picture albums to prison with you. Which is where you're going if we don't get the hell out of here."

Eddie grabbed her suitcase, zipped it up. His mother snagged two bottles of Jim Beam from a cabinet on the way to the truck. Eddie threw her suitcase in the back beside his bag, and they both climbed inside. Seconds later, they were tearing out of the trailer park. The barn was at the back of Eddie's uncle's property a couple of miles away. His uncle was a drunk just like his mother. The man never stepped foot in the old barn anymore—he mainly just sat in his beat-up recliner, watching old Westerns. His uncle lived off a settlement he'd gotten after an injury working on an oil rig. He had no idea Eddie was currently using his building for a kidnapping.

"You sure about this, Edward?" the old lady asked.

"What? The girl?"

"Yeah. Let's just leave her and go."

"Hell no! I already made a call. We'll be able to live off the money we can get for her down there for a long time. I ain't going down there to be broke."

"All right. I'm just nervous about the border."

"We'll hide her on the floor in the back seat. I ain't worried."

Eddie pulled off the main paved road and found a dirt driveway on a wide-open property. There was a little white house off to the right where his uncle lived. But Eddie kept straight on a dirt road that led to a couple of acres behind the house where a big metal barn stood. He pulled up to the barn, and they both got out. After sliding open a barn door, Eddie and the old lady went inside.

The barn had six stalls for horses, an open space in the middle, and several storage rooms along the right side. There were no horses. His uncle had stopped caring for horses a few years back. The barn mostly sat empty. The girl was locked in the last storage room, where she'd been kept for the past several hours.

The old lady sat on a bench and opened one of the bottles of whiskey. She quickly downed a big gulp. Eddie had no doubt his mother would be passed out for most of the drive south. That was probably a good thing. He didn't want to listen to her yap at him about how badly he'd fouled all this up. She'd started off that way when he'd first called her but quickly shut up when he threatened to leave without her. He knew she would eventually start back up again.

"You tell Beth to hurry?" the old lady asked.

"Yeah, but you know Beth. Still, I told her we would leave her if she didn't get her ass here on time."

"We ain't leaving her."

"I know that. I just needed her to get moving."

Eddie thought he heard movement outside the barn. Was Beth already here? He was going to be shocked if she'd packed and gotten her things here so quickly. Eddie walked over to the barn door and pulled it open. When he did, he stared directly into the long barrel of a gun with a silencer. He didn't recognize the guy holding it. Small in stature, black ski cap, gray running suit. There was no way this guy was with the FBI or the police. He was clearly not there to arrest him.

He was there to kill Eddie.

And probably the old lady, too.

It was over.

THIRTY-EIGHT

Dani followed Lars Kingston's black Bentley away from Zilker Park, where he'd privately met with lawyer Nelson Wyatt. Then she trailed him for about an hour as the wealthy man made several peculiar stops. First to a flower shop, where he came out with a bouquet of pink roses. Then a jewelry store, where he walked out with a small package. Finally, Dani trailed him on foot into a Whole Foods grocery store, where he purchased an assortment of chocolates and cookies. Dani wondered what the hell he was doing. Lars had to know by now that his youngest son had just been shot and killed. The police were beginning to notify the family when she was leaving the crime scene earlier. But instead of heading over in that direction, Lars was running around town and buying gifts like it was Valentine's Day. Who was this all for? His wife? Someone else?

Back inside her car, Dani followed Lars out of the grocery store parking lot. Her phone buzzed with a new text message. Her boss, Simon. I'm sorry for the way this went down today. Maybe the time off will be good for you. And for us, too. Dinner tonight? She sighed, shook her head. Unbelievable. Simon was probably not going to want to still have dinner with her when he found out she'd disobeyed his direct orders.

Lars drove all the way through downtown proper and then pulled off in a parking lot under Interstate 35 near the river. He parked his Bentley all the way up under the highway bridge in the darkest part of the lot. Dani pulled her Mazda to the edge and watched from a distance. The parking lot was mostly empty. Only a few random vehicles. There were several dirty camping tents around where the homeless had set up shop nearby. What was Lars doing here? He did not get out of his car. A few minutes later, a black Ford Taurus pulled into the same parking lot and settled right next to the Bentley. Lars immediately jumped out of his car and rushed over. The back door of the Taurus opened, and a young girl got out.

Dani's jaw dropped. Piper Slater. Jake's daughter. *What the hell?* The girl and her grandfather immediately embraced. The Taurus then quickly backed out. Dani took a quick mental snapshot of the license plate. As the sedan passed by her to exit the parking lot, Dani got a good look at the face of the driver. Logan Gervais. Dani cursed. Did the hit man have Jake's daughter this whole time? That didn't make any sense. Gervais hadn't even arrived in Austin until this morning. Could Lars have somehow been behind Piper's disappearance? She didn't think so—not from the look of relief that poured across his face when his granddaughter appeared.

Lars opened the passenger door on his Bentley and helped Piper inside. The gifts were clearly for his granddaughter. Piper looked to be OK. No visible physical injuries, from what Dani could tell from this distance. Where had she been? If Gervais was involved, did that mean someone else was now dead? Someone Lars had discovered had taken Piper? How was this connected to Steve and the shooter at his house?

Dani's first instinct was to stop Lars from leaving and start asking questions. But Lars could have already been informed that she'd been removed from the case. She probably wouldn't get very far. He'd just ignore her. She decided to keep following him instead. While Piper was likely safe with her grandfather, Dani had this growing sense that everything was about to go down. Jake was looking for his daughter, and now she was under the care of Lars Kingston.

Could Jake be very far behind?

Could his own daughter be used as a trap against him?

THIRTY-NINE

Beth Spiller lived in a small but picturesque yellow house surrounded by an eclectic mix of other colorful houses in a funky part of South Austin. Jake pulled up in his truck just in time to find Beth outside in the short driveway, frantically shoving suitcases in the back of a white Ford Explorer that was parked under a carport. Beth was clearly on the move. She was getting out of town. Had her brother told her what had happened with Steve?

Jake figured he had two options: Stop her from leaving and threaten her until he got some answers. Or follow her and hope she might take him directly to Piper. Both carried risk. If he confronted her, Beth might shut down and not give him anything. And it was not like Jake had a gun where he could threaten violence if she wasn't helpful. But he might somehow lose her out on the streets if he tried to follow her. Then he'd be left with nothing. Jake had to make his decision right now. Beth was getting into her Explorer and getting ready to leave. If he was going to stop her, he needed to pull into her driveway right now and block her. He decided not to do that, with the hope that Beth might lead him straight to Piper. That's all he wanted right now. To find his daughter and get her back.

Jake ducked down in his seat as Beth backed into the street and then drove away. Then he popped up, did a quick U-turn, and closely followed her. He could not worry about being noticed. It was riskier to get caught at a red light. Beth was driving fast. She was clearly in a hurry. Jake had to do some quick maneuvering in and out of traffic along South Congress to keep up with her. Then she turned onto Highway 71 and headed east. Was she going to the airport? He would have to stop her before she got on a plane. But she did not turn into the airport. She kept going on 71 until she pulled off and started following a couple of lonely, isolated ranch roads on the outskirts of East Austin.

Beth was driving over eighty miles per hour now. She was quickly zipping around slower cars. Jake had to be careful, keeping up but not being so close that Beth might notice he was behind her. He didn't want to tip her off. A few more turns here and there, and then Beth was driving onto a property with a long dirt driveway leading up to a small white house. Jake slowed along the main road. Beth did not pull up to the house; instead, she followed the dirt driveway around back to where Jake spotted a big metal barn. His heart jumped. *Piper!* She had to be inside the barn.

Jake pulled into the driveway and followed the same dirt path. He could see a truck with big tires parked right outside the barn. Someone else was already here. Eddie Cowens? He had to presume. The guy probably had a gun. How would Jake make his move, up against a weapon? He didn't know, but that wasn't slowing him down. His adrenaline was spiking. Beth was already out of the Explorer. Jake pulled over into the grass so he wouldn't get too close and put her on alert. He opened his door, got out, and began hustling as quietly as possible toward the barn.

The scream he heard come from inside the barn stopped him cold in his tracks. And it wasn't just one scream—it was continuous screaming. Someone inside was in absolute hysterics. Jake took off running full speed toward the barn. His whole body was pulsing with fear. Was it Piper? Had something happened to Piper? Without hesitation, Jake raced inside the open barn door. Beth was on her knees in the dirt in the wide-open space of the barn in front of him. She wailed uncontrollably. Stepping forward, Jake could now see why. Eddie Cowens was lying on his back in front of her, blood completely covering his face. There was a hole square in his forehead.

The guy's eyes were open, but he wasn't moving an inch. Just beyond Eddie was another person down. This was an older woman. She was lying sideways on the ground, but it also looked like she'd been shot through the head. Both were clearly dead. Absolute terror gripped him. Was Piper dead, too? Was he too late? Had he broken his promise to always be there for her?

Jake ran over to Beth, grabbed her forcefully by the arm. She seemed startled by his sudden appearance, as if she hadn't even heard him enter the barn.

"Where's my daughter?" Jake yelled at her.

Beth was sobbing and barely able to respond. "I . . . don't . . . know."

Letting go of Beth, Jake raced over to each of the barn stalls, but there was no sign of Piper in any of them. He then rushed over to what looked like storage rooms. He yanked the first door open. It was filled with stacks of old bags of horse feed. A second room had a workbench and metal shelves lined with junk. No Piper. Jake went for the last door. He noticed a lock and chain lying in the dirt right in front of the door. Jake grabbed the handle and pulled the door open. *God, please.* But Piper was not inside. The room was empty except for one wooden chair and an old camping cot. There was a blanket and pillow on top of the cot. And there were a couple of fast-food bags wadded up on the dirty floor next to the chair. Piper had to have been kept inside this room. But where was she now? Who had killed Eddie and the other woman? Had they also taken Piper?

He returned to Beth, who was still hunched over her dead brother. She looked up at him. Beth was still crying hard but had caught her breath a little.

"Do you know who I am?" Jake said, kneeling in front of her.

She nodded. "I'm . . . so . . . sorry."

"Who did this?"

"I don't know. I was supposed to meet my brother and my mother here to leave the city together. But I don't know who could've done this to them."

"They had my daughter here?"

She nodded. "Yes."

Jake wanted to unload all his anger on this woman, but he knew that wouldn't do him any good right now. Beth probably would crumble on him. He needed to stay calm to get information out of her. "Beth, I need you to tell me the truth about everything. Right now."

"I didn't mean for any of this to happen. I swear. It just . . . it kept escalating until everything spiraled out of control."

"You've been having an affair with Steve Kingston?"

She seemed reluctant to answer.

"Answer me!" Jake screamed at her.

"Yes! For about eighteen months. He was supposed to leave his wife. He promised we would get married this next year."

"Was it your brother who killed my wife in the car wreck last year?"

She bit her lip. More tears hit her eyes. Then she nodded.

"Why?"

She visibly swallowed. "Steve had taken a lot of money from the firm. Sarah discovered it and confronted him with it. She said she was going to tell their father. Steve thought he was going to lose everything. He thought his father might turn him in to the police and send him to prison—that's how much Steve believed his father hated him. Steve had been supporting me financially. The house, the car—all of it. I told my mom and my brother what was happening. If Steve lost everything, that meant me and my family would also lose everything. That's when Eddie decided to take matters into his own hands."

Jake tried to process that. "Steve wasn't behind what happened to Sarah?"

She shook her head, wiped the tears from her face. "It was Eddie. I should've stopped him, but I didn't. I'm so very sorry."

"What happened last night at Caitlin Kingston's house?"

"Eddie was working the birthday party yesterday at the Kingstons' place. I guess your daughter somehow recognized him from the night of the car wreck. Steve told me she took a picture of him on her phone and told Caitlin, who shared with her father and Steve what was going on—that your daughter thought Eddie might be the same man who was involved in the hit-and-run accident. I panicked and told my mother. Eddie didn't mean to shoot Caitlin. He was just trying to scare them. The gun accidentally went off. Then my brother freaked out and grabbed your daughter because she saw the whole thing."

Jake's head was spinning. "Did Steve know Eddie took my daughter?"

"No. Steve didn't know about *any* of this until a few hours ago, when I finally told him the truth."

"What did Steve do?"

"He was devastated and so angry. He said he had to go talk to his father. To make it right. Then he told me to get out of town."

"Have you talked to Steve again?"

She shook her head. "He won't return my phone calls."

It dawned on Jake that Beth had no idea her own brother had executed her lover. It must've been his one last desperate attempt to salvage the dire situation. But it hadn't worked. And now their own dead bodies were piled on top of the others because of it. If Steve had gone to Lars and told him the truth, could Lars have sent someone here to this barn? Jake thought about the man who had tried to shoot him in the park and had killed Brent Grisham instead. Dani had mentioned that a hit man had been hired to kill him. Could that hit man have been hired by his father-in-law?

When Jake had threatened to expose Lars's affair during the custody battle earlier this year, the first words out of his father-in-law's mouth were, "You're a dead man, Jake. I'll have you killed." Jake had dismissed it at the time as an overly emotional response to their heated situation. But could Lars have chosen this moment to follow through with it? Did Lars see it as an opportunity to finally get rid of Jake altogether?

Jake suddenly stood. "I have to go."

Beth looked up at him with the saddest eyes. "What do I do?"

"Call the police. Tell them the truth. It might just save your life."

FORTY

Jake drove fast back across Austin. His emotions were swinging on a wild pendulum. On one hand, he felt a hesitant relief at the possibility that Piper might actually be in safe hands—even if those were the blood-covered hands of his crazy father-in-law. Piper being OK was all that mattered to him. On the other hand, he was mad as hell. Lars Kingston had created a toxic family culture where money, power, and pleasure—and the protection of all three—were at the center of their entire world. A dark world that had damaged his own children in so many crippling ways. As Lord Acton said, *Power tends to corrupt, and absolute power corrupts absolutely.* Steve had fallen victim to it. The dominoes that tipped over in the aftermath were devastating. Three members of the Kingston family were now dead—along with many others. And if that wasn't bad enough, Lars had decided to take everything to the next level by bringing in his own hired gun. If it were up to his father-in-law, Jake also would be dead right now. And then Lars would finally get what he'd wanted from the moment Sarah had died—Piper.

But Jake wasn't going to let that happen. He'd been thinking about where his father-in-law might have taken Piper, assuming she was now with him. Jake doubted Lars would simply drive her back to his estate up on the hill. The whole family was probably there, and now in even more despair because of Steve's death. Lars would want more control over the situation. He would want time to manipulate the entire narrative around how he'd somehow gotten Piper back himself. To make sure his hands were clean with all that had happened. His father-in-law owned a secluded house on heavily wooded acres that backed up to Lake Austin.

Jake had been there only one time. Two months after Sarah had died, Lars had asked to meet with Jake privately. It was there that Lars had made his first request—or demand—that Piper come live with them instead of remaining with Jake. That conversation didn't go well, of course. And things had gone from bad to worse from there. Jake didn't think even Janice knew about the house. It wasn't decorated as if she had been involved. There were no frills. The modern glass house was bare bones furniture-wise and felt more like a man cave for someone super wealthy. Jake figured that was exactly what it was. A place off the map where Lars Kingston had his private sexual trysts and affairs.

Once back in West Austin, Jake followed the winding path of Westlake Drive as it cut through the hills near the river until he finally arrived at a gated driveway surrounded by trees. Jake had no idea what the code for the gate was, so he parked the truck just outside. Then he climbed over the gate and began to quickly make his way down a driveway covered with gray-and-black pavers. The house was not visible through the trees from the road. Jake wondered if the hit man who had killed Eddie Cowens and his mother could also be at the house. Would Lars keep a guy like that around as added protection? While Jake desperately wanted to have his daughter back, he also needed to be careful.

Jake finally reached a point in the driveway where he could see the two-story white stucco house with black trim in front of him. Directly behind it were the waters of Lake Austin. Jake paused, searching. There were no cars parked out front. But he would expect Lars to use the three-car garage.

The completely private house had expansive windows throughout, front and back. Jake began looking window to window. So far, he didn't see any movement inside. Maybe he was wrong. Maybe Lars hadn't brought her back here. But then he spotted the man suddenly move past the expansive glass-front entry. Jake's heart started beating even faster. Piper had to be here, too. He could think of no other reason why Lars would be at this place all by himself on a day like today.

Jake stayed near the tree line but carefully began approaching the house. His eyes continued to search window to window. There was no sign of his daughter yet, and no sign of anyone else being at the house other than his father-in-law. Which gave Jake the confidence to approach boldly. It was time to end this right now. It was time to get his daughter back. He hustled up the rest of the driveway and then peeled off on the walkway up to the huge glass front doors. One more quick peek around inside the house. No Piper in sight. If she was here, where was she? He was about to find out.

Jake banged on the door. Seconds later, Lars appeared in the foyer and froze when he spotted Jake standing there. Jake could tell by the look on the man's face that his father-in-law was shocked to see him. Was the front door locked? Would Lars even answer it? Or would Jake have to find a way to break in? He got his answer a moment later when Lars finally stepped up to the door, unlocked it, and then opened it before blocking the entrance with his big body.

"What the hell are you doing here?" Lars said.

"Where is she?"

"I'm calling the police right now."

"Do it!" Jake yelled at him. He could feel every emotion he'd been carrying around inside him for the past several hours rise to the surface. The fear, the panic, the desperation. It began pouring out. "Because I can't wait to tell them how you hired a hit man to find me and kill me. A killer who has left a trail of dead bodies throughout the city. You're going to prison, Lars. I'm going to make sure of it!"

"You're a lunatic. They'll never believe you over me."

"Where is Piper?" Jake repeated.

"She's not here. Get off my property."

"You're lying. Get out of my way!"

Jake moved toward the door, but Lars didn't budge. There was no way Jake was going to allow this man to slow him down. Not after everything he'd been put through to get here. So Jake punched his father-in-law as hard as he could in the gut. It felt good. The man let out a grunt and doubled over. Jake rushed past him into the house and started searching. There was no one in the study or a guest bedroom. The end of a hallway led him into a spacious master suite. The lights were off in the bedroom, and the shades were drawn. Someone was under the covers in the king-size bed. Jake's heart was on the verge of exploding. He rushed over to the bed. *Piper.*

She was asleep. Jake stood there for a moment as every emotion he'd been holding on to so tightly rushed through him. He'd found her. He'd kept his promise. She was safe. But he knew they had to get out of there. Jake gently nudged her awake, so as to not frighten her. His daughter's eyes fluttered open. When she recognized her father standing over her, Piper lunged at him with both arms. *"Daddy!"*

Jake pulled her in close, holding her so tightly. Tears flooded his eyes as a powerful relief he'd never experienced before flowed through him.

FORTY-ONE

Dani had followed Lars Kingston back to a secluded house near Lake Austin. Because she'd been suspended, she had no real authority to directly confront the man. So she parked just up the street and tried to sort out her game plan moving forward. She wanted to be careful that her engagement with this matter didn't jeopardize the FBI's official investigation. Wealthy people with powerful attorneys had ways of ripping holes in investigations in court. If Lars was behind the hiring of Logan Gervais, as she suspected, she didn't want him getting away with it on a technicality. But then, in her rearview mirror, she noticed a white truck suddenly park right outside the gated driveway. A man got out. Dani perked up. It was Jake, and he was in a hurry. Jake quickly climbed over the security gate and rushed up the driveway. Something big was about to go down. Dani knew she couldn't tap-dance her way around this anymore.

She reached for her phone, called Mitchell.

"How're you doing, Dani?"

"I'm sending you a location. I need a team here ASAP."

"What's going on?"

"I'll explain when you get here."

"But you're suspended."

"Just get over here, Mitchell!"

Dani hung up, climbed out of her vehicle, and raced over to the gate.

FORTY-TWO

"Are you OK?" Jake asked his daughter.

He couldn't stop hugging her. They had their arms tightly wrapped around each other. Over the past several hours, he'd tried so hard to not think about how he'd even go on with life if he lost her, but the dreaded thought constantly hovered just below the surface. To finally release it from his mind was surreal.

"Yes, just really scared. What is going on, Daddy? Grandpa won't tell me anything."

"You're safe now. With me. But we need to get out of here right away."

"OK. But I really need to go to the bathroom."

"Go, but be quick."

Jake hugged her tightly again. Then he watched her hurry into the master bathroom. Stepping out of the bedroom, Jake was eager to find a phone and call the police himself. He didn't want Lars driving off and then trying to grab a private jet out of the country. The man had the means to go hide anywhere. He wasn't going to let Lars get away. While his father-in-law wasn't responsible for Piper's abduction, Lars's actions had caused the deaths of several other people—and nearly Jake.

When he returned to the living room, he found himself once again standing in front of his father-in-law. Lars hadn't tried to leave. Instead, he was taking a different approach. One Jake hadn't anticipated since he'd never known Lars to own a weapon. But now, Lars had a gun in his hand and was aiming it directly at Jake.

Jake stiffened. Had he come this far only to be stopped by a bullet from his bitter father-in-law? Had he risked everything just to have it end this way? He couldn't let this happen. "Don't do this, Lars. Please. Piper is in the next room."

"I should have done this a long time ago. Sarah deserved so much better than you."

The man had an unstable look in his eyes. One Jake had never seen before.

"I loved your daughter. And she loved me. Sarah would not want this."

"Piper should be with us. Not you."

"This isn't the answer. Hasn't this family seen enough death? Sarah. Caitlin. Steve."

Jake's mention of Steve's death seemed to jar Lars. His forehead bunched, and his eyes started twitching, like he was having a difficult time processing it. It dawned on Jake that the man didn't know his youngest son was also dead. Lars must've been ignoring his phone for the past hour.

"This has to stop," Jake said. "It's over."

He watched as his father-in-law's face pulsed red with rage. "It's over when I say it's over. Not you." He was not putting the gun down. If anything, Lars was clutching it even tighter. The man had lost any sense of reality. He was so far over the edge now. Jake looked around for a way to defend himself. He was too far away from Lars to make a move for the gun. If Lars wanted him gone, finally and forever, Jake could do nothing about it.

But then a familiar voice boomed out from the kitchen. "Put the gun down, Mr. Kingston!"

Lars spun around. Jake was stunned to see Dani swiftly approaching, her own gun drawn in both hands, aimed directly at his father-in-law. Where had she come from? How had she known?

Lars froze but didn't put the gun down. He still held it in his hands, as if considering his situation. Dani moved within ten feet.

"Put the gun down, sir," Dani repeated. "I will shoot you."

Still, Lars didn't relinquish his position. He seemed on the verge of making a desperate move. Would he still try to shoot Jake? Dani? Himself? But then Lars heard another voice. One that seemed to hit him differently.

"Grandpa?"

Jake turned. Piper was standing at the entrance of the living room.

Piper's eyes quickly watered. "Grandpa, what are you doing? Please, stop."

And that's when Lars's arms suddenly went limp, as if accepting reality for the first time. He dropped the gun to the floor. Then the man fell to his knees, put his hands to his face, and began to weep heavily.

Dani rushed over, kicked the gun away. Jake grabbed Piper, pulled her in close to him as his daughter continued to cry. He looked over at Dani. They locked eyes and gave each other a brief nod of gratitude. Nothing more needed to be said. They had been there for each other when they'd needed it most. Jake glanced out the front windows and noticed a group of FBI agents racing up to the house with their guns drawn. Dani was already on the phone with someone, barking out orders.

Jake exhaled. Maybe for the first time in hours.

It really was over. Finally.

FORTY-THREE

Three months later

Jake and Piper held hands while walking the trails near Auditorium Shores along Lady Bird Lake in the heart of Austin. It was a beautiful, sunny early-spring day. They had both just indulged in ice cream cones from a vendor truck up the way. Piper had her favorite—cotton candy with sprinkles. Jake stuck to his usual plain vanilla. They were celebrating their move back to Austin. Jake had just driven a U-Haul truck into town last night. They were renting a house in North Austin until he could hopefully buy something soon. He wanted to plant roots again. He knew Piper needed it. In so many ways, they were completely starting over as a family. And that was OK.

The past three months had been a difficult time as they'd tried to recover from her traumatic abduction and the fallout from so much death and chaos in the family. Jake had immediately been cleared of all charges. Beth Spiller had told the police the truth. She was remorseful but would still do plenty of jail time. Lars had stubbornly lawyered up and was now awaiting trial. But there was too much evidence that he was behind hiring a hit man who had killed several people. All his money and power would not save him this time around. Lars would likely be going to prison later this year.

There had also been some positives to what happened. The rest of the Kingston family had embraced Jake more in the past three months than the fifteen years prior, as if the dark truth about Lars had finally set them free. He would not be able to dominate and control them from a prison cell.

Jake knew they had a long road ahead of them—maybe a lifetime. Piper was still regularly having nightmares. Jake would often wake to find her snuggled up in the bed next to him. Which he welcomed. He hardly wanted to be away from her for even a second. Both of them were regularly seeing a therapist. Jake had been completely honest with his daughter about everything that had happened. She needed to know the truth about the secrets that had nearly destroyed her mother's family in order to fully heal. But the dark cloud that had hung over the two of them since Sarah had died seemed to have lifted, finally. Despite the challenging circumstances, Piper seemed to be happy for the first time since all this had begun.

Jake was happy, too. He'd gotten a coaching job at a local middle school. It had felt so good for him to be back on the football field working with kids again. He was slowly getting his life back. And maybe something else.

Dani sat in her car and took a deep breath. She was surprised by how nervous she felt. While she and Jake had regularly been talking on the phone for the past few months, she had not been around his daughter yet. At least not outside her official FBI duties. She really wanted Piper to like her. That was probably dumb, but she couldn't help herself. She was also nervous for other reasons. It felt surreal to be talking to Jake again. Even though it had been fifteen years, they had so easily slipped back into a natural rhythm. She'd had a lot of extra time to talk on the phone with him since she'd had to serve out a thirty-day suspension. Did she really want to go down this road with Jake again? The first time had ended so painfully. She had to accept some blame for that. She'd chosen to go to DC. He'd chosen to stay. Dani had wanted to blame it solely on Sarah Kingston all these years, but it was clear in talking it through with Jake recently that it was never about Sarah.

One more deep breath.

Was she ready for this? To put her heart out there again?

There was only one way to find out. She got out of her car.

Jake paused near the statue of Stevie Ray Vaughan, the legendary singer-songwriter.

"What are you doing?" Piper asked.

"I told you. We're meeting someone here."

"Oh yeah. Why won't you tell me who it is? What's with the secrets?"

Jake smiled. "You'll see."

About that time, Dani walked up to them from the opposite direction. She wore a burnt-orange UT hoodie, black leggings, and running shoes.

"Piper, you remember Special Agent Nolan?" Jake said.

Piper nodded. "Hi, Agent Nolan."

"Hi, Piper. You can call me Dani, OK?"

"Oh, OK, sure. So you're the big surprise guest?"

Dani glanced at Jake, who shrugged and grinned.

"I guess so," Dani said. "Surprise."

Piper rolled her eyes in a playful way. "Come on, Dad. I saw this coming from a mile away. You *hate* talking on the phone. But you've been on it nonstop for months."

"Guilty as charged." Jake laughed. "I just wanted you to have a chance to get to know each other better. Is that cool?"

Piper looked back and forth between Jake and Dani. She was thirteen. She obviously knew what was going on here. Jake wasn't sure how Piper was going to react. It was probably a lot for her to think about her father bringing a new woman into his life. She'd been through so much. He certainly didn't want to do anything that might disrupt her recovery or their newly reestablished father-daughter relationship. This was the first test.

His daughter smiled. "OK, cool."

Piper turned to run off toward a grassy area.

But Jake stopped her. "Hey, Piper!"

She looked back at him.

"You and me?" Jake asked.

She grinned ear to ear. "Always."

Then she began practicing her tumbling in the grass.

"Well, that was easy," Dani said to Jake.

"I'm glad. I really didn't want this to stop."

He smiled at her. She smiled back. While they had agreed to take things slow, Jake had to admit it already felt like they were right back in their twenties. They just fit—they always had. While he certainly didn't regret the direction he'd taken back then because it ultimately led to having Piper, Jake was excited about a second chance with Dani. The past year had been so dark. But the future was looking very bright.

"Hey, guess what?" Dani said. "We finally got him."

"Who?"

"Logan Gervais."

"No kidding?"

"New York grabbed him first thing this morning."

"That's great news."

Logan Gervais had disappeared off the map immediately after things had unraveled in Austin three months ago. But Jake knew the FBI had been in full-on hunting mode. He had to admit he felt relieved to know the dangerous man was in custody. Maybe the nightmares about him would finally stop.

Jake took a deep breath. He thought about Sarah. At some point, he knew he had to move forward and truly start over. She would want that for him, and she would want that for their daughter. So he said a final goodbye in his heart. And then he reached out his hand toward Dani. She hesitated a moment but then placed her fingers in his. And they began walking toward Piper together.

ABOUT THE AUTHOR

Chad Zunker is the Amazon Charts bestselling author of the stand-alone novel *Family Money*; the David Adams series, including *An Equal Justice*, which was nominated for the 2020 Harper Lee Prize for Legal Fiction, *An Unequal Defense*, and *Runaway Justice*; and *The Tracker*, *Shadow Shepherd*, and *Hunt the Lion* in the Sam Callahan series. He studied journalism at the University of Texas, where he was also on the football team. Chad has worked for some of the country's most powerful law firms and has also invented baby products that are sold all over the world. He lives in Austin with his wife, Katie, and their three daughters and is hard at work on his next novel. For more information, visit www.chadzunker.com.